# STARS AND SIGNS

"It is warm inside, my dear. Let us take some air." Orion steered her toward the tall glass terrace doors.

"Oh, but I am not overwarm," Artemis said.

"You are flushed," he insisted. "And I wish to speak with you."

He pulled her through the doors and over to a more private spot near the low stone wall that enclosed the high terrace. The moon was just past full and the scent of the faded autumn foliage wafted up from the dim garden far below.

"Having fun, my dear?" he asked.

"Yes. And what is so important that you must drag me out here? And since when do you call me 'my dear'?"

He shifted so only she could see his face.

"Since when? Since you resisted my efforts to bring you out here quietly . . . and since the entire ballroom is now staring at us . . . and since I would wager there are among them at least one or two who can read lips." He moved closer to her and lowered his face over hers.

"What are you doing?"

"They think we are quarreling. I am changing their minds."

He stole a kiss . . . and her eyes closed, heavy-lidded with desire . . .

# BOOK YOUR PLACE ON OUR WEBSITE AND MAKE THE READING CONNECTION!

We've created a customized website just for our very special readers, where you can get the inside scoop on everything that's going on with Zebra, Pinnacle and Kensington books.

When you come online, you'll have the exciting opportunity to:

- View covers of upcoming books

- Read sample chapters

- Learn about our future publishing schedule (listed by publication month *and author*)

- Find out when your favorite authors will be visiting a city near you

- Search for and order backlist books from our online catalog

- Check out author bios and background information

- Send e-mail to your favorite authors

- Meet the Kensington staff online

- Join us in weekly chats with authors, readers and other guests

- Get writing guidelines

- AND MUCH MORE!

**Visit our website at
http://www.kensingtonbooks.com**

# LORD LOGIC AND THE WEDDING WISH

## MELYNDA BETH SKINNER

## ZEBRA BOOKS
### KENSINGTON PUBLISHING CORP.

http://www.kensingtonbooks.com

ZEBRA BOOKS are published by

Kensington Publishing Corp.
850 Third Avenue
New York, NY 10022

All Kensington titles, imprints and distributed lines are available at special quantity discounts for bulk purchases for sales promotion, premiums, fund-raising, educational or institutional use.

Special book excerpts or customized printings can also be created to fit specific needs. For details, write or phone the office of the Kensington Special Sales Manager: Kensington Publishing Corp., 850 Third Avenue, New York, NY 10022. Attn. Special Sales Department. Phone: 1-800-221-2647.

Zebra and the Z logo Reg. U.S. Pat. & TM Off.

First Printing: February 2003
10  9  8  7  6  5  4  3  2  1

Printed in the United States of America

*For Kathryn Rose,*
*whose logical mind soars with*
*imagination and loving-kindness,*
*and who makes her mama very proud.*

# Acknowledgments

This is my third novel, and I'm having a blast. Part of the fun lies in thanking those who have helped me out. This time, I wish to express my gratitude to my first editor, Amy Garvey; my brand-new editor, Hilary Sares, who stepped in midway on this project; my literary agent, Jennifer Jackson; my critique partner, Mary Louise Wells; my trusted readers, David Andrews and Erma Andrews; Horace and Frances Skinner, a two-person sales force majeure; Chris Andrews, whose pride in my work makes me smile; Kathryn Rose and Julie Rain, who take great interest in my stories and who help me wherever they're able; my own very logical husband, Barry, who wisely knows that reason and joyful inattention can coexist; and the lovely Regency fans who took the time to write me concerning my first two books.

You're all a dream come true.

# PROLOGUE

*West Sussex, England*
*1799*

He had waited all year for this.

The idea had come to him one day last summer, when he was still but seven and his governess was making threats concerning the eating of peas. Orion had thought about his idea all summer, all autumn, as he waited for the first good snowfall. Today was the day. There were six and three-quarters inches on the ground. It was cold. Cold and windy.

As he plowed—*chuff-chuff*—through the white, his nose hurt and his eyes felt dry, but his feet still carried him gladly toward the river. There wouldn't be anyone else outside in weather like this. No, they'd all be inside, singing and smiling and draping green stuff all over the place.

That's what was going on back at Stonechase Manor, and that's what would be going on throughout the countryside. All the children would be inside, making kissing boughs or ivy wreaths. All the adults, too.

But not Orion. He couldn't wait to escape all that buffle-headed nonsense. He couldn't wait to be by himself, to be outside. Today, the outside belonged to Orion. No one around to stare or snicker. He could turn over stones and logs all he wanted, and no one would even know.

Beneath his green woolen scarf, he smiled.

The wind had subsided by the time he reached the river, and he knelt next to one of the huge, bare lindens that had been planted all over the estate long ago by one of his ancestors, the first Earl of Lindenshire. Orion pulled from under his coat a hand spade he'd purloined from the gardener a few days ago. With it, he cleared the snow within the V of two great black roots, taking care not to disturb the earth beneath.

As he worked, he thought about the inherent injustice in an earl being made to eat those wretched peas. Nasty tasting things! He'd had to eat them last week, too. What did it matter that he was only eight years old? An earl still shouldn't have to eat such things if he didn't want to.

He was so intent upon what he was doing that he didn't notice the girl near him until her head of dark, glossy curls popped up out of the blanket of white snow a few yards away, nearly scaring the bubble-and-squeak out of him. Orion's heart leapt into his throat, and he almost gave a scream.

A *girlish* scream.

In front of *her*—Artemis.

That would have been a disaster. He gripped his spade tighter and pretended not to have noticed her. She sat up. He turned his head until she was almost but not quite out of his line of sight, way off to one side. She watched him for a moment and then spoke.

"Hello, Orion."

He pretended not to have heard her.

"I *said*, 'Hello, Orion.' "

Orion looked up into the tree, as though he'd heard

an owl or perhaps a dead leaf rasping against the bare boughs.

"Hmmph!" She stood up and walked a few paces away. Orion thought she was going to leave, and he was sorry without really understanding why he should be. But then, quite suddenly, she sat down and lay back in the snow once more.

He stopped what he was doing and stared. Her black clothes stood out against the snow, and as he watched, she extended her arms and legs and waved them parallel to the ground.

"What are you doing?" he asked, forgetting he wasn't supposed to have noticed her.

"Making snow angels."

"I can see *that*," he said, irritated. "But this," he said, gesturing around him, "this is my experiment place. Why are you doing that here? And why now?"

She shrugged. "Don't know. Destiny, I guess."

"Destiny?" Orion frowned.

"Fate."

"Fate!" Orion scoffed. *Destiny . . . fate . . . what rubbish!* Gypsy rubbish, he supposed. He'd heard the servants talking about her grandmother. The old woman was a Gypsy, a fortune-teller. She could read palms and see omens, they said. Orion didn't believe in all that nonsense, and he didn't understand how the adults could, either. He knew he was just a little boy, but he also knew what made sense and what didn't.

Artemis stood and moved to another location, lay down, and waved her arms and legs again. Orion's fingers clenched and unclenched around his spade.

"There. Ten. Should be enough," she said, getting up and brushing the snow from her ugly black mourning clothes. Her father, a nice man who had taken the two of them fishing once or twice, had died a month ago.

"Enough what?"

"Enough angels. They are going to watch over my boat."

"What boat?" Orion said, getting really irritated now. She wasn't making sense—not that *that* was anything unusual. Artemis didn't usually make sense, but she didn't usually laugh at him, either, which is why he put up with her silliness. While she sometimes poked fun at him for other things, she was the only one who didn't laugh at him for thinking too much. She never laughed at his experiments, and she liked to listen to the songs he made up.

"I am launching this boat," she said, picking up what appeared to be little more than a bundle of sticks. "What are you doing?"

"I am digging to see if there are any insects crawling around under the snow in the winter."

"Oh," Artemis said with a polite nod, though he knew she didn't have any interest in his bugs. "Well? Are there?"

Orion shrugged. "Don't know. I haven't looked yet. You disturbed me," he accused.

"Sorry." Artemis knelt at the side of the river. It had begun to freeze over, and she broke apart the thin layer of ice near the edge with a fallen branch. Then she pulled from her pocket a small packet made of paper folded into a neat, white square.

"What's that?" Orion asked, coming closer, unable to stem the tide of his own curiosity.

"An envelope."

"I can see *that!* What's in it?"

"A wish."

"Huh?"

"I wrote a wish and put it inside." She tucked the envelope between two sticks and then pushed the little boat into the current and watched it float off.

"What did you wish for?"

"I can't tell you that," she said, turning and crinkling her nose up and giving him a look that suggested he was the stupidest boy in all England. "If anyone but me finds out what my wish is before it makes it to the sea, the wish won't come true. Don't you know anything?''

"Rubbish." Orion scoffed again. "Superstitious rubbish. How can you believe in all that Gypsy nonsense?"

"It's not nonsense."

"Is too."

"Orion Chase, you are smart, but you don't know anything."

"Hah! Do so. I know you are silly to believe in all that wish and destiny and omen and fortune-telling rot," he said smugly.

"It isn't rot. Mama told me it's real. She pretends she doesn't believe in it because Papa's family would be cross if she didn't, but she really does, and she's right. It is real. It's real, and I will prove it!"

"Never in a thousand years. Silly girl."

She scowled. "Ooo! You . . . you . . ." she sputtered, casting about for a suitably despicable insult.

"Earl?" he supplied with a smug grin, knowing it would enrage her. Waving his title in front of her nose always did. Her mama was the daughter of an earl and a Gypsy, and Artemis was always complaining about how unfair it was that her mama—an only child—couldn't inherit the title.

"I was thinking *prig*," she answered.

"Shouldn't that be, 'I was thinking prig, *my lord*'? You Gypsies are all alike, always forgetting your place."

She looked daggers at him for a moment and then curtsied. "I beg your pardon, Lord *Logic*," she finished and stomped off, her breath leaving behind little clouds of warm vapor as she walked, her feet squeaking against the snow with every angry step.

Orion grinned and watched her disappear over the hill. He always enjoyed provoking her, and he was sure he'd not seen the last of her that day. Her mama and his were friends, and they always saw a lot of each other. Their houses were perched atop neighboring hills. If he looked hard enough, Orion could see the light in

Artemis's window at night. Yes, with all the Christmas festivities, he'd be seeing more of her later on, he was sure. Thinking no more of her, he turned back to his experiment.

First, he cleared a new hole in the snow, reasoning that the old one had been exposed to the cold too long; any insects there would have crawled or flown away by then. Carefully turning over some dead leaves, a branch, and some rocks, he discovered several insects, but they appeared dead.

The loamy smell of the exposed earth filled his nostrils as he gently put the insects into a small, clear glass bottle. He corked the bottle, then set out for home. Were the insects dead? Or were they only sleeping, like bears did in the winter? Would they come back to life as soon as he got them warm by the fire?

He paused to tuck the little bottle into the deepest pocket of his brown woolen coat. It wouldn't do to have one of the adults see it on the way to his room. They'd confiscate it, he was sure.

He almost missed the wish-boat.

At the last moment before he cleared the steep bank, he glanced down at the half-frozen river, where a patch of darkness stuck out against the background of snow. It was Artemis's boat. It had run aground against the near bank a hundred feet downstream, caught in a tangle of dead plants like a fly in a spider's web.

Orion frowned. The puny little stick boat would never make it to the sea. Likely, the thing wouldn't make it any farther than right where it was. But Artemis didn't know that.

He looked down at her footprints, where they led off through the winter woods toward her father's land. What if she came back to check on her boat? She'd be disappointed that her stupid wish couldn't come true, wouldn't she?

Orion rolled his eyes. "Silly girl," he said, but he scrambled back down the sloping bank and trudged downstream to pluck the boat from its sticking place. He looked at the thing, taking note of its too-low prow and too-narrow beam. There was nothing to keep the boat parallel with the current. No keel and no rudder. No ballast, either.

Artemis didn't know the first thing about shipbuilding. If the boat hadn't become stuck, it would definitely have capsized. He shook his head, and, tucking the boat under his arm, he headed for home. No, the boat would certainly never make it to the sea, but Artemis didn't have to know that. He liked her—not that he wanted to, well, to *kiss* her or anything—and he reckoned this wish nonsense would vex her. It might even make her cry.

Girls cried a lot.

Back at Stonechase Manor, Orion sneaked up to his bedchamber with his precious insects. Ridding himself of the boat, which he carelessly tossed onto his dressing table, he sat upon the gray stone hearth and pulled the insect bottle from his pocket, his fingers trembling with excitement.

And Artemis's wish-boat? It lay forgotten until a maid noticed the mess of dirty twine and sticks the next morning and disposed of it in the fireplace.

The wish envelope, however, escaped the boat's grim fate. The envelope had skidded across and over the edge of the polished surface of the dressing table and fallen into an open trunk, where it lay lodged out of sight behind the trunk's green satin lining.

Orion didn't even realize the little square of paper was missing. There were too many other mysteries to occupy his logical, ordered eight-year-old mind. Yes, he forgot about the little boat and the wish envelope entirely, though he never quite forgot Artemis.

The little girl with the black curls moved from her

father's estate and away from the neighborhood that very day, quite suddenly and without farewells, but the memory of her laughing eyes and teasing mouth stuck with him through the years.

# CHAPTER ONE

*West Sussex, England*
*1815*

Artemis sat down on the ledge of an arching gray stone bridge and looked at the bottom of one smarting foot. A sharp stone had finally broken through the leather sole of her left boot. That made two holes, and she wasn't even halfway to London yet. She plucked the stone from where it was lodged and looked eastward down the lane she was traveling.

The narrow track ran through a grove of sturdy pear trees heavy with golden, sweet-smelling fruit. Beyond the grove, the fields were hedged in yew and crisscrossed with tidy gray stone walls. This part of England, south and west of London, was often amazingly green even into November, and for a moment she allowed herself to fancy what it would be like to stay here in this place. Staying anyplace for more than a fortnight would be heavenly, but here . . .

Below her, the brook sparkled and splashed in the slanting rays of the afternoon sunshine. Blue butterflies

browsed here and there among the buttercups, and
birds trilled to each other. Everything was green and
golden and fragrant, and she inhaled, filling her lungs
with color and sound as much as she did with the crisp,
cool air.

She'd forgotten how beautiful it was here.

Climbing wearily to her feet, she wondered if she'd
ever see it again. London lay fifteen leagues to the north-
east, at least three more days' walking. Once she found
a position there and sent for Anna, she wouldn't be
taking many pleasure trips.

She walked between the tracks so the grass would pad
her tired feet. Who was she bamming? She'd *never* be
taking any pleasure trips. Not anymore.

She could remember going to Brighton when she was
very young, back when Papa was alive and she and Mama
were still welcome at Branleigh. She looked to the north,
trying to catch a glimpse of her childhood home, but
couldn't spot Branleigh's brick through the thick leaves
of the pear trees.

It was no matter. Some years ago, her grandmother
had died and the estate had passed to a distant cousin
of hers. Artemis doubted anyone there even knew who
she was.

She looked away. A moment later, a dove cooed
nearby, directly in her line of sight toward Branleigh,
and her eyes strayed toward it once more.

A low rumbling far behind her heralded an approaching carriage. She gave way fleetly, stepping off
the lane and between two rows of pear trees. The coach
slowed as the four blacks pulling it climbed the bridge
and then picked up speed as they came down the other
side.

As the coach passed her at speed, she heard a lady
within laughing gaily, and then, with a curious jingling,
two *somethings* sailed out the coach window in twin
flashes of blue. One of the objects landed right at Artemis's feet, and those in the coach rolled on, oblivious—

or uncaring—of the loss. She suspected the latter, since she could plainly hear the woman singing a rousing rendition of "Greensleeves."

Artemis looked down. On the dark green grass at her feet lay one of the most outrageously ornate stockings she had ever seen. It was enough to make even a Gypsy blush. Their white cotton knit was trimmed with row upon row of blue lace, splashes of blue and silver silk embroidery, short silver tassels, and—most amusing of all—a dozen tiny silver bells. The bells jingled merrily when Artemis lifted the thing. How strange that such a thing should fall right at her feet!

Was it a sign?

What did it mean?

The thoughts occurred naturally to her. The signs, after all, were always there, if only one looked, and Artemis did. The signs guided her, comforted her, kept her from harm. She wondered which they were doing now. What were they telling her?

She looked around. The air was heavy with the lazy warmth of late afternoon. The western sky was beginning to glow orange, and the deepening shadows were slanting lower and lower. A flock of sparrows had settled en masse into a nearby pear tree, where they noisily vied for the best perches to pass the night upon.

It would soon be time for Artemis to seek her own place to roost for the night. She'd thought to continue on to the next village and beg a spot on someone's hearth or, at worst case, to sneak into someone's hayloft. But the next village was still two leagues away.

Is that why the stocking had come to her? To help her decide what to do, where to seek shelter? She turned it over, looking for an answer, and the bells jingled once more.

She shook her head in wonder at the cascade of tiny silver bells. Why, they were well nigh Romany! She'd seen such things on Gypsy scarves or skirt hems. But why would anyone, Gypsy or not, sew bells to their—

Bells!

Her eyes found the second stocking and widened. It had come to rest a few yards into the grove. If she drew an imaginary line from herself to the stocking, the line would pass right through the Stonechase estate. Stonechase Manor, where lived the widowed Countess of Lindenshire. Belle Chase was her name, and Artemis laughed. Of course! The dove—a symbol of peace and friendship—the bells, the position of the second stocking . . . surely they were signs, signs that were meant to guide her to her mother's old friend.

For a moment, she thought about ignoring the signs for once and trudging onward. After all, Lady Lindenshire could hardly be expected to remember Artemis after all these years, and it would be entirely too humiliating to appear at the door in need. In the end, need won out. Artemis was tired and sharp-set, and the prospect of a warm bed and a full belly was too much even for pride to render insignificant.

She finally struck off down the lane at a brisk pace. She had a distance to travel before she dared leave the lane and set off toward Stonechase. She'd have to skirt Branleigh entirely. Even though no one there would remember her now, she doubted she would be welcome, and an unpleasant encounter would spoil the memories she kept locked in her heart, happy memories of her mama and papa.

It was close on sunset when Artemis approached the sweeping front of Stonechase. The gray fortress of a house was not beautiful, but she looked up at it lovingly anyway. She'd spent so many happy hours there as a child in the company of her mama or of Orion, Lady Lindenshire's son. They'd had the run of the place, along with the ever-present chimney swifts.

Her heart beating hard, she knocked, and a few moments later the dour-faced Stonechase butler opened the door. In the east, the sky was an inky blue, and stars had begun to appear, while in the west, the heavens looked as though they had been set on fire. The pink light made the butler's snow-white hair appear pink, too. Artemis grinned.

"May I help you, miss?" the butler asked, quickly assessing her appearance.

Something about his expression seemed familiar. She ransacked her memory. "Mr. Peabody?"

His eyes narrowed. "And you are?"

"Artemis Rose." She dropped a curtsy and grinned, suddenly and unaccountably filled with pleasure. "How lovely to see you again! I am so pleased."

"Miss Artemis Rose?" he said, squinting at her. "Upon my honor, miss!" he exclaimed. "You cannot be half as pleased as I am. Wait until her ladyship hears you are arrived! I daresay she shall be twice as pleased as both of us! Follow me. No need to announce you. She'd likely flog me for making you wait," he said, though the chuckle he gave belied his dire prediction.

It took no time at all to be admitted to the evening parlor, a comfortable room dominated by earthy browns and creams, bold patterns, and sturdy old furniture. It was not the sort of room in which Artemis would have expected a wealthy countess to find her leisure. Instead, she'd imagined the countess in a room full of delicate, uncomfortable chairs and pale yellow silk, crystal and gilt. But those, apparently, were not the sort of surroundings Lady Lindenshire found comforting. She had been sipping tea and reading a book here, curled up on a plump brown sofa near the fire.

"My lady, pardon the unexpected intrusion, but I was certain you would not wish to wait a second more. Presenting—"

The teacup and book lay forgotten, and the older woman rushed forward even before Artemis's name left the butler's lips.

"Oh, of course I know who you are! I would know

those eyes anywhere. They are just like your dear mother's. Where is she?'' the countess asked, glancing eagerly behind Artemis.

The countess was a striking woman. Tall and straight of stature without seeming austere, she moved with an honest grace. She was dressed simply but elegantly in soft peach-colored muslin. Her hair was a lustrous golden brown, and her brown eyes were set in a lightly lined plane, revealing a face that smiled often.

*Just like Mama*, Artemis thought, *always smiling*. She wasn't surprised. Belle Chase and Artemis's mother had been bosom friends throughout their girlhoods.

''Lady Lindenshire,'' Artemis said, dropping a curtsy, ''I am afraid I have sad news to impart. My mother died eleven months ago.''

Instantly, the lady's brown eyes darkened, glistened with tears, and glazed over for a moment with her own private pain before refocusing once more and returning to Artemis. ''You poor dear,'' she said at last in a quavery voice. ''I . . . I loved your mama very much and was simply heartbroken when she . . . when you were forced to . . .'' She gave a delicate shudder. ''Pray accept my sincerest condolences.''

''Thank you, Lady Lindenshire. Your sincerity could never be in question. I feel I know you, for Mama spoke most highly of you until the very day she died.''

The countess gave her a sad, yet grateful smile. ''How did she . . .''

''It was sudden,'' Artemis averred. ''A fever.''

Childbed fever, to be precise, but Artemis was unprepared to explain about Anna. Though her mama really had admired her friend Belle Chase, what little firsthand knowledge Artemis possessed of the countess had been gathered through a child's eyes. Her memories of the lady were all pleasant ones, to be sure, and yet . . . and yet in spite of her own recollection and her mother's regard, Artemis still couldn't be sure how the countess would take the news of Anna's birth on the wrong side of the blanket.

The countess sank wearily to a seat on a brown damask sofa. Motioning for her to sit, she asked, "What brings you here, my dear?" Her intelligent brown eyes took in Artemis's travel-weary Gypsy clothing and threadbare portmanteau, cataloging every detail. Nothing missed her scrutiny: the lopsided red felt hat Artemis wore, the heavily embroidered yoke of her close-fitting shirt and full black skirt, the red scarf she wore about her waist, and finally, the tired old brown boots. It was a frank and unapologetic perusal, though her expression was kind. She didn't try to hide her curiosity, and the distaste Artemis could spot from a furlong away was absent from Lady Lindenshire's still beautiful face.

With sudden certainty, the grown-up Artemis decided she liked Lady Lindenshire as much as the little-girl Artemis had.

"Have you been to Branleigh?" the countess asked lightly, though Artemis detected a certain wariness in her eyes.

"No, ma'am."

She made a clucking noise. "I thought not. I am afraid you will find little welcome there, should you venture it. Your cousin, the current master of Branleigh, is an old man set in his ways and not very fond of visitors, be they family or otherwise. Do you have alternate lodgings for the night?" Her eyes flicked to the window, probably expecting to see a gaudily painted wagon and a flock of motley Gypsy folk. To her surprise, Artemis fancied she saw a flash of disappointment in the lady's eyes at finding the forecourt of Stonechase Manor devoid of any such tableau.

Artemis couldn't help smiling. "I have come alone, on foot, and I have no place to pass the night. But I had reason to hope you might be so kind as to rectify that shortfall." She explained about the amazing stockings she still had tucked into her bag.

"Ah," said the countess, "so you are following the portents, then? Just like your mama always did." She gave a wistful smile. "A lovely woman, your mama. Glossy hair the color of a lump of coal, the fairest skin, and eyes the color of the sky. Your papa fell in love with her at first sight, you know." She sighed and then looked at Artemis. "And you, my dear, look just like her."

"Just like who?" a deep, resonant voice interjected from the doorway. A large man sauntered into the parlor. He had straight, nut-brown hair and eyes to match. For one mad moment, Artemis thought he might be Orion, and her heart gave a leap.

Even after all these years, the thought of seeing Orion Chase again brought with it the same mixture of joy and dismay it had when they were children. He'd been both her closest playmate and fiercest rival.

She watched the man advance to a place before the wide oak mantel. The coloring was right, and there was something familiar about the eyes, but the gentleman wore no spectacles and was dressed in what she supposed was the height of fashion. A bottle green coat with a daffodil-embroidered silk waistcoat beneath and an expertly tied cravat topped black Hessians with a mirror-like shine and breeches so tight she wondered how many valets it took to pull them on. They showed every bit of muscle the man possessed—and there was a great deal of that to show.

He was no pudding-bodied dandy, but a sporting man. Tall and broad-shouldered, the muscular gentleman shouldn't have been able to move with any sort of grace, but he did. He looked more like he was dancing than walking as he glided to a stop before the countess and gave an elegant bow. No. This definitely wasn't Orion, she decided. A close cousin, perhaps. Her heart settled, as a startled bird soon folds herself back into her nest.

"Just like who?" the countess echoed. "Why, only turn to see for yourself." She waved toward Artemis, and the gentleman pivoted. "Does she not look just as her mother did so long ago? Or do you not remember her? You were awfully young, Orion."

"Orion?" Artemis blurted and turned toward the countess. "This is your son, Lady Lindenshire? The one born on the same day as I?"

The lady nodded, and the gentleman bowed. "Lord Logic at your service once more," he said. His waist still bent, he looked up at her, and an impish smile played about his mouth and eyes—the same impish grin that had pricked her temper a thousand times before.

"It is uncommonly good to see you again, Gypsy."

He was Orion, sure as the signs. Her heart gave another leap—and then plunged lower than a whale's belly, for her situation seemed only that much worse. It was embarrassing enough having to apply to Lady Lindenshire for a meal and a bed, but now, with *him* here—

He was staring at her, waiting for her to say something.

She gathered her dignity—or as much of it as she had left—and said, "I . . . I hadn't imagined you would be in residence, my lord."

She had imagined him married and living at one of his other estates. In her travels, she had seen three others. Stonechase was the smallest of the lot.

"The fashionable time to appear in Town is past, and the earliest of the Yuletide house parties will not commence before another week. Does our meeting displease you?" he asked.

"By no means! I am very glad to see you again, my lord." *In spite of my utter humiliation,* she amended to herself.

"Why so Friday-faced at my appearance, then? You were hoping my bed would be empty so you could use it, perhaps? I fancy we *may* have another bed somewhere. No cause for dismay." His dimples grew deeper, and he crooked an eyebrow. He was toying with her, as he had done so often when they were children. The scoundrel must have overheard her plea to his mother for a bed, and he wasn't going to leave the matter alone, as any true gentleman should. No, he was going to needle her about it.

He was quick and intelligent and ruthless—and a gentleman.

She relaxed, knowing intuitively that Orion was attempting to relieve her embarrassment in the only way he could. To make no mention of her desperate circumstances would have done nothing to help, but to make fun of it . . . he was the only person in the world who could have gotten away with it, and it worked beautifully, for her embarrassment was set to nought.

"Has my appearance startled the words from your head, Gypsy?"

"Well," she said, trying hard not to return his mischievous smile, "your appearance was rather startling, my lord. Your physical appearance, that is, for I am a little disconcerted with how you have grown."

He puffed up, proud as a peacock, as she expected he would. As children, she had remarked upon his intellect, but she certainly hadn't complimented him for his scraggly boyish looks—not that he had cared one fig or even noticed the discrepancy. As a young man, however, he would be pleased to be noticed, and he had good reason, after all.

"I suppose I *have* become taller and broader in the intervening years," he said with obvious pride.

"Oh, no," she said, shaking her head and pasting on a deliberately perplexed look. "No, that is not it at all. In truth, you look much the same as you did long ago." His expression fell, and she pounced for the kill. "I should have recognized you immediately but for your startling lack of skinned knees and spectacles. Not even so much as a snake hanging from your pocket. Apart from those things, I would have known you. You have not changed."

"Oho!" Lady Lindenshire laughed. "Parry and riposte. Touché, my dear." She turned to Orion. "You had best be on guard while Artemis stays with us."

Orion turned to Artemis, his eyes dancing. "And how long will we have the pleasure of your company, Miss Rose?"

"Pray, I do not think I can bear such formality from you. I am and always have been Artemis. I give you leave to use it."

"Very well." He nodded. "And you will call me Orion, I trust?"

"Indeed. Unless I call you 'Lord Logic,' that is."

A smile passed between them, like a rare warm breeze on a cold afternoon, and Artemis wished she could stay for more than one night. It would be grand to pass a few days in the Lindenshires' company. She found the countess just as her mother had so often described: warm and merry. She couldn't help wondering what it would be like to get to know Orion through the eyes of an adult.

Reluctantly, she turned herself from such thoughts. "I will be taking advantage of your hospitality for only one night. I must away to London as soon as I can. I . . . I have an engagement there that cannot be put off." In truth, there was nothing awaiting her in London. Instead, a baby girl awaited her back in a dilapidated old wagon encamped outside of Truro. But there was no need to tell her hosts any of that. What good would it do?

"Only one night?" the countess exclaimed. "Do not say so! Orion, you must help me persuade her to stay longer, at least a fortnight. I will tolerate no less."

Orion smiled at Artemis. "One day *is* much too short a time to renew an acquaintance, and my mother and I would both enjoy your company. Your presence has breathed life into this dreary time of year. Please do say you will delay your departure." He grinned. "If you will not, I cannot be responsible for the result. My mother is a most persuasive woman."

Artemis rather thought Orion had the market on persuasion all buttoned up. At that moment, it seemed he had all the stars in the sky in his eyes, along with all the sincerity and soulfulness in the world. She had forgotten how appealing he could be. That much, at least, had not changed.

The mantel clock ticked away the seconds, and Artemis considered their plea to remain for a few extra days. It would be all too easy to say yes, to linger in this golden country in their company, to pretend, for one last, precious moment in time, that she belonged somewhere. She hesitated a moment before shaking herself out of such foolish reverie.

Anna needed her now, and that was that.

"I cannot stay any longer than one night, my lord— Orion." She smiled. "I really came only because of the stockings."

"Stockings?" Orion asked.

"Two stockings flung from a passing coach," Lady Lindenshire explained.

"Just as I was passing Stonechase."

"They aligned perfectly." Lady Lindenshire nodded.

"And led me to seek you here."

"It was a sign, Orion. They pointed Artemis right to us. Thank goodness she followed."

Artemis waited for Orion to flash another one of his amazing smiles and nod his understanding. But as he listened to the story, the earl did not break into a smile. In fact, his face clouded over and darkened until Artemis wouldn't have been surprised to hear thunder.

His rather sudden change in attitude did not escape his mother, either. "Orion, you look as though you have tasted sour pickles. What is the matter?"

Orion turned haughtily toward Artemis. "Am I to understand you are still living as a Gypsy after all these years? Traveling and sleeping in a wagon?" He swept her attire from bottom to top, taking in the loose, flowing black skirt she wore, the fine cotton chemise, the scarves. His eyes widened, as though only just then seeing her clearly. "I had hoped you had changed. I see now I was wrong."

His sudden disdain shocked her—and then anger gripped her. "As of a week ago, I have no home whatsoever, wagon or otherwise. I am on my way to London to procure employment as a serving maid or seamstress or anything else that will pay me enough to—" She was going to say *to support my baby sister,* but stopped just in time. Any mention of Anna would bring on a barrage of uncomfortable questions. "Enough to live on," she finished. "I have been traveling on foot, and I have been sleeping in haystacks."

Orion scowled. "You mistake the source of my disapproval. It is not your Gypsy way of life that disappoints, but your Gypsy beliefs. I had thought you would have abandoned such nonsense along with your pigtails."

"And I had thought that you would have abandoned your dogged skepticism along with your spectacles. You, my lord, possess no objectivity. You cling to illogical bias."

"Illogical? You do no not know the meaning of the word. You are as senseless as ever."

"And you are as ill-mannered as ever."

"Children!" Lady Lindenshire exclaimed.

"Ill-mannered? Oho! The pot is naming the kettle black, then, isn't it, Gypsy?"

"Hardly."

"Come now," he said, "you cannot imagine I approve of your manners, can you?"

"Your approval or lack of it matters not one whit to me. Arrogant man!"

"Children! Please"—the countess placed one hand on Artemis's arm and held the other out to Orion—"please be calm."

Orion straightened and pulled his heels smartly together. "I am calm, Mama. I am calmly walking out the door and calmly leaving you ladies to your chat."

He turned to Artemis. "Good day to you, Miss Rose. I hope you enjoy your stay here at Stonechase Manor and that your road into London is smooth. It should be lovely weather tomorrow. Perfect for traveling." With a curt bow, he was gone.

"The ass!" Artemis said, forgetting for a moment that Lady Lindenshire was present.

"Indeed!" the countess said. "Stubborn, too."

Artemis whipped her gaze around to meet the older woman's, surprised at the lady's rather vehement concurrence. "He has not changed at all. He is still priggish."

The countess nodded. "And much too intelligent."

"And too opinionated."

"Quite." The older woman held out a cup of tea to Artemis and smiled. "You like him."

Artemis took the cup, sat, and flicked a small smile back at her hostess. "Indeed."

The countess laughed. "The two of you were always that way. Oil and water. Inseparable, but always separate, repelling each other even as you moved together. Louisa and I had hoped the two of you might . . . ah, but it was not to be. You and Orion were at odds from birth, it seemed. The entire countryside knew early on you would never suit. Louisa and I never gave up, but I see now it is hopeless. It seems you bring out the beast in him, for I assure you, my dear, my son is *always* a perfect gentleman. Except for today, that is." She shook her head and gave a wry smile.

Artemis looked at her hands. "Was it always so?"

"Oh my, yes!" the countess said. "Always. From the day you were born, you brought out the beast *and* the best in him, it seemed. He was always happy when you joined him in his ramblings and always smiling when he returned."

"Except when he was scowling?"

Lady Lindenshire laughed. "Precisely. I told you: oil and water."

The two lapsed into silence for a few moments, and Artemis thought about the man Orion had grown to be. There was much to admire: a keen intellect, a delightful sense of humor, and there was no use denying the purely feminine reaction she had to his appearance. With his broad shoulders and considerable height, his quick, perfect smile and his friendly eyes, Orion would look well in rags. Dressed as he was, he cut a very fine figure indeed.

She knew little of the current fashion, but she recognized quality. The clothing he wore was very expensive, and it showcased his manly proportions to a nicety. Orion Chase had become a stunningly attractive man, and no woman in her right mind could fail to see that.

"I wonder," Lady Lindenshire said idly, "if you and my son had got on better as children if your father's family would have been so quick to cast you off."

It was a bold, well nigh rude thing to say, and Artemis looked at the countess sharply.

"Oh, dear," the older woman said. "I have spoken too plainly. Forgive me, my dear. You look so like your mama that for a moment I forgot . . ."

Her kind eyes held no trace of animosity or ill grace.

Artemis waved her hand dismissively. "I do not mind in the least. Friends speak to each other with openness and honesty. I am not my mama, but I prefer plain speaking, just as she did, and I give you every leave to speak the same way to me as you did to her."

Lady Lindenshire nodded. "Done." She sipped her tea thoughtfully.

"Is there a new Lady Lindenshire?" Artemis asked. "If so, I should enjoy meeting her before I leave." It would be very interesting to see what sort of woman Orion had taken to wife.

"No," the countess answered, "My son has not yet married, drat him. As far as I have seen—and much to my annoyance—he has not yet begun to look for a bride, though I hear rumor of his having shown some interest in a certain young lady this past summer. But even if it is true, nothing came of it. The lady in question has married, and Orion has said nothing of it. It is high time he found another lady, I vow, for he owes me grandchildren!''

''He is but four-and-twenty,'' Artemis said gently. ''There is still time.''

The countess dimpled. ''Yes, of course . . . but I am impatient. More tea? And—goodness, my dear!—I have forgotten my manners. Are you hungry?'' Without waiting for a reply, she went on. ''Pray sample these lovely biscuits Cook made, and I will ring for something more substantial.'' She pressed a biscuit into Artemis's hands. ''Now, about your staying here for only one night . . . I have an idea. I travel to London soon, and a number of my servants will precede me to make ready for my arrival. They depart in two days' time, and you, if you wish it, may travel in the coach in their company.''

''Why,'' Artemis exclaimed, ''that would put me in London a day or two earlier than if I walked the remaining distance!''

''Precisely. And we would be able to enjoy the pleasure of your company for another day.''

''Oh, Lady Lindenshire, I am only too happy to accept!''

''Good! And, of course, I will write you a reference. I daresay with my recommendation you can do much better than serving maid, my dear. And I insist you agree to stay at my house in Town for as long as it takes to procure a suitable position.''

''Oh,'' Artemis said on a sigh, ''thank you so much, Lady Lindenshire!''

''Nonsense,'' the countess said. ''It is my pleasure. And you must call me Belle!''

''Belle.'' Artemis nodded happily.

Their conversation turned to other things. As they chatted happily, Cook provided a delicious meal of cold chicken, warm bread, three kinds of cheese, with ale and an exquisite pear tart. The countess picked at a small portion to be polite, while Artemis tried not to eat too much and failed miserably.

Midnight approached, and they were both fighting yawns as they reminisced about Artemis's mama. She missed Mama very much, and it was comforting to talk to Belle, who really had loved Mama dearly. Artemis hated to see the night end, but finally, after she'd yawned thrice in one minute, Belle sent her off to bed with the promise of more time to talk on the morrow.

A maid showed Artemis to a magnificent room, much like the one she remembered occupying at Branleigh. As a footman filled a hip bath, the young maid delivered a soft cotton nightrail that probably belonged to Lady Lindenshire, for it was much too long for Artemis. Her dusty garments were soon whisked away to be washed, and Artemis was left alone.

Outdoors, November's chill nipped the air. She thought of Anna asleep in the Gypsy maid Isabel's arms. The wagon would be cold this night. Artemis trusted Isabel to keep Anna warm, but still she wished the little girl could be here enjoying this lovely fire.

Artemis looked about her. The room was large and held a clothespress, a huge four-poster, a dressing table, and a window seat. The polished wood floor was covered with a thick, blue carpet, and the walls were hung with blue and gold patterned paper and lovely gold draperies. How Anna's eyes would fill with wonder at a room such as this one.

She heaved a sigh. It was unlikely Anna would ever see such a fine room, unless she were cleaning one.

Ah, well . . . there was no sense in mourning over that which could not be changed. As Artemis bathed, toweled dry in front of the glowing fire, dressed in the soft nightrail, and finally slid between the crisp, clean linen on the bed, the optimism that came to her naturally took over. It was best to focus on the good things. She would not have to walk to London with holes in her boots, she would have a place to stay while she found a position, and she would have a very influential letter of reference. Everything was going to work. She could feel it.

She had forgotten what a real bed felt like, and she stretched luxuriantly, savoring the sleepy minutes before she fell asleep. Once again, the signs had led her where she needed to be. It seemed she'd found a friend in Belle Chase.

If not for Orion, everything would have been perfect.

# CHAPTER TWO

Artemis couldn't quite wrap her mind around the changes that had taken place within and without Orion. Though he had changed on the outside, he was much the same inside, she fancied. And that which *had* changed did not seem to fit with what hadn't.

He'd been a curious little boy, forever exploring and minutely examining the world around him, and logical to a fault even then. She remembered that he would become fiercely annoyed with behavior he saw as illogical, and, since people often did things that made no sense, poor Orion had isolated himself.

That part of him, at least, had changed. He'd become a man of fashion, his mother had told her—more than that. He was a regular tulip, to hear her tell it. And apparently, he was often in London attending balls, salons, musicals, picnics, balloon ascensions, the opera, and routs. So, somehow he must have shed his desire for social isolation. Lady Lindenshire's account made it sound as though he'd turned completely around. According to her, he didn't just gingerly, judiciously partake of Society's offerings; he basked, wallowed, reveled in them.

And yet he wasn't looking for a wife. Why?

Judging by Orion's intensely negative reaction to the story of how the signs had led Artemis to seek his mother—something that he could not fit into his neatly ordered concept of how the universe functioned—finding a wife was going to be difficult. There couldn't be very many ladies in the upper ten thousand so intensely interested in fashion and so fiercely dedicated to the accepted laws of science and the pursuit of knowledge.

It was an odd combination of interests.

But what had she expected? Orion had always been odd.

She forgave him his earlier outburst. She had provoked him, after all.


The afternoon sun was veiled behind a thick blanket of gray clouds. Orion and Artemis had gone for a walk about the grounds, which were filled with workers. It was the height of the pear harvest.

They had come to the ruins where they used to play as children, and Artemis sat, watching Orion climb atop the jumble of stones. As she had known it would, Orion's temper had cooled. He had apologized quite sincerely that morning at breakfast, and he'd acted as a gentleman should ever since. Yet Artemis could see he had adopted a certain reserve where she was concerned.

He was cordial, however, and even gave free reign to his curiosity about life in a Gypsy caravan. He had questioned her at length about it that day, and their conversation had filled several pleasant hours. It had been a warm and pleasant day, in spite of the dreary clouds.

"I am relieved," she remarked, watching as he leapt confidently from stone to stone.

The sky was gray and the wind had risen. It whistled

through the lindens and sent autumn's spent leaves bouncing and wheeling over the meadows. In the orchards, the workers were singing, their voices reaching the ruins on the wind.

Orion stopped what he was doing and regarded her thoughtfully. "Relieved?"

She gestured toward the pile of rubble beneath him. "Yes . . . well, when I first arrived yesterday, I thought you'd become too high in the instep for such things as climbing the ruins. You are so clearly a man of fashion these days." Even now, on their walk, he was elegantly attired in a bottle blue coat, silver waistcoat, and expertly tailored black breeches. "You look like you should be paying a morning call at some famous lady's salon rather than rambling over the countryside with a Romany maid."

Orion gave a comic bow from atop the rubble. Beneath him, a great slab of ancient, brown-stained stone teetered. He nearly lost his balance, corrected, and then cocked a self-assured smile at her. "There is no one I would rather impress than you."

She laughed. "Perhaps that is because there is no one else around."

He shrugged and smiled. "Nothing escapes you," he said impishly.

She looked down at her clothes. "I am afraid my own garments do not compare favorably to yours. We must be a curious sight." She had on the same black skirt, red-embroidered chemise, and boots as yesterday, but she had made an effort to modify the costume by pinning her hair up, rather than letting it flow loosely over her shoulders, as usual. And, though she was still wearing a scarf, it was the blue one, and she was wearing it as a shawl instead of tied about her waist. "I am afraid I would be thrown out of a fancy London salon." She laughed.

"Even so," he said with a nod, "I would not dishonor

you by conducting myself with any less decorum than I usually do.''

"You always dress this way now?"

"I do." He nodded.

She watched him for a moment. As he stepped with surefooted confidence from one giant piece of rubble to another, his golden brown eyes scanned the jumble of lichen-covered stones. Suddenly, he stilled and bent his head to one side. As his eyes narrowed to peer into the deep shadow under a slab of marble, his face took on a serious cast.

At once, she realized he was looking for bugs or some other crawly things. She well nigh laughed. Here he was, the dashing young Earl of Lindenshire, a paragon of good taste, a man who had obviously dedicated himself to the pursuit of a fashionable existence, and yet at least one corner of his mind—or more, judging by the look of concentration on his handsome face—was still much concerned with beetles and salamanders.

They were still within distant view of the orchards, but the farther they'd ranged from the house and the more distance they'd put between them and other people, the more relaxed and open he'd become.

He hadn't changed one whit, she realized. Not on the inside, at least, but on the outside . . .

"Why?" she asked. "Why do you always dress that way?"

He paused and met her gaze. Pressing his generous mouth into a straight, heavy line, Orion appeared to be framing an answer, but then he looked suddenly toward the horizon. "I believe a storm is coming," he said. "We should return to Stonechase."

He climbed down, tucked her arm in his, and set off.

He had also neatly changed the subject.

Orion was obviously uncomfortable talking about himself, and Artemis wondered about that, too, but she decided to let the matter drop—at least for the time being. She didn't want to spoil their time together with any further unpleasantness. She was having a lovely time at Stonechase. And Orion was everything that could be expected from an attentive host and friend.

In fact, thus far, she would have found him a most pleasing companion but for the fact that he had ignored her whenever she spoke of the signs—which, of course, was often. Any mention of portents had him veering off on another subject if they were sitting together—or veering off on another footpath if they were walking together. It was quite annoying. As logical and as intelligent as he was, Orion couldn't see what was right in front of his nose—a lack that had nothing to do with his ridiculous refusal to wear his spectacles.

She discovered he was still quite long-sighted when they returned to the house.

"The woods and fields are as lovely as I remembered them," she said. "Thank you for the tour."

"I had a lovely time escorting you, in spite of the dreary weather," he said. The sky was now hopelessly overcast with dark clouds, and the rain that had been threatening since yesterday seemed imminent.

"Do you play chess?" she asked.

He looked at her speculatively and then shrugged. "Not much. Boring."

"Boring?" she exclaimed. "Then I daresay I think you do not truly understand and appreciate the game."

"You misunderstand," he said, his eyes dancing with mischief. "I meant only that the game is not challenging enough for my own enjoyment, for I always win."

"Indeed!"

"Do you play?" he asked.

"Well," she said carefully, "I would not call what *I* do 'play,' my lord. I am quite serious about the game."

"Oho! That sounds like a challenge."

She inclined her head and smiled. "I suppose I would not mind . . . *instructing* you for a game or two."

"By Jove! Instruct me, will you? I see. Perhaps we both have something to learn, then."

She laughed. "If you can teach me anything, Lord Logic, I would welcome the opportunity." The game was afoot, and they strolled toward the east parlor companionably until they reached the gallery.

The room was long and narrow, with a cavernously high ceiling. No window that might admit damaging sunlight broke the smooth planes of the green-papered walls, though the room was indirectly lit from sunlight that streamed into the rooms it connected. Artemis stopped to admire one particularly fine likeness of one of Orion's ancestors. The high walls were full of portraits, large and small, for the family had been very wealthy even before the first earl.

The portrait was of a young woman dressed in an old-fashioned gown. The eyes bore a resemblance to Orion's, a striking golden-brown and keenly intelligent, but the hair was well nigh white-blonde, and the woman was petite. Artemis wondered who it was.

Most of the frames had tiny golden nameplates attached. She squinted at this one.

*Twin Sister,* it read. "This must be one of your great-aunts. I remember them from when I was a girl. They seemed quite ancient."

"They were. They both died in my tenth summer, aged ninety-and-seven."

"Very respectable. Which one is she?"

Orion leaned forward and peered minutely at the nameplate. "Georgianna," he pronounced, as though he were reading the name.

Artemis gave a most unladylike bark of laughter. "You cannot see!"

"What?"

"You cannot see! I had thought your eyes improved themselves with maturity, but that is not it at all. You are simply too proud to wear your spectacles."

Orion looked annoyed—and confused.

She skimmed her fingers over the nameplate. "There

is no name here. It says only *Twin Sister*. You only pretended to read the name. Admit it.''

Orion's strong jaw line set solid, and he said with tight formality, ''For once, Miss Rose, even I cannot deny the logic of your conclusion.''

He moved toward the parlor at a brisk pace, and Artemis hurried to catch him. ''But why?'' she asked. ''I understand vanity, but why lie to me, of all people? Surely you have no interest in impressing me.''

He stopped next to a tall window in the next room, a small parlor done in green. He looked down at his hands, and his jaw worked. Somewhere, a clock chimed the hour of four, and Orion blinked, then blew out a small, forceful sigh. ''Forgive me, Artemis. It was not my intention to lie to you. It was . . . force of habit.'' He clasped his hands behind his back. ''I have a certain reputation to maintain among the *ton*. I am much in London, and spectacles are not . . . not part of my Town image.'' He hesitated for a moment, as though uncertain of his next words, but finally he said. ''It is very simple, really. Nothing more to tell. End of story.'' He pulled his watch from his pocket and strode off, looking at it, almost seeming to have forgotten her.

It was obvious to Artemis there was a great deal more to tell. And then, at that moment, the sun broke through the clouds, limning his brown hair with a halo of golden light.

He stopped and turned to look at the sky. ''Amazing! I thought those clouds were impenetrable.''

Artemis smiled and shook her head. ''I am not amazed at all. I know it for what it is: a sign.''

Orion's lip curled. ''A sign—bah! What rot!''

She motioned to the watch in his hand. ''Beneath the smooth face of a watch lies a complex mechanism, hidden away in the dark and difficult to discern. That break in the clouds, the light streaming in upon you— it is a sign that things are indeed more complex than you let on." *And,* she added to herself, *that it is my responsibility to expose your inner workings to the light.*

He scowled. "You are speaking nonsense."

She shrugged. "Then that makes two of us. You choose not to see clearly."

He threw two exasperated hands in the air and, grasping her arm, propelled her toward the parlor. "Come lose at chess, Gypsy." To her relief, he did not seem angry, just annoyed.

"You might be surprised," she said. "Gypsies love chess. We invented it."

"Ah, but you are not a Gypsy. Not a true Gypsy."

His words stung, and she winced.

He stopped and gave her a questioning look. "I say, have I managed to put my foot in it?"

"Please understand," she explained, "I have heard those same words hundreds and hundreds of times since . . . since . . ."

"Since your father's family so cruelly turned you and your mama from your rightful home?"

There was sudden, white-hot anger in his words that quickly contracted and cooled into a sober, clear hatred. Artemis was stunned—and profoundly grateful. "Thank you for your depth of feeling, Orion, but I choose not to focus on that part of my past. I rarely think about Branleigh anymore, and I hold my cousin blameless. That part of my life was only eight short years. The next sixteen were much more important and have had more lasting effect. I have lived the life of a Gypsy all these years—I *am* a Gypsy! I speak Romany, I cook Gypsy food, dress in Gypsy clothes, and dream Gypsy dreams. But," she said with a shrug, "I have never truly belonged there, in caravan. I was never fully accepted anywhere, and neither was my mother."

Orion looked puzzled. "I know your mother was not accepted at Branleigh because her mother was a Gypsy, but why did the Gypsies not accept her?"

"My mother's father was not Gypsy. The way the Gypsies view it, half Romany is also half Outsider. And, of course, my own blood is only one-quarter 'pure,' as they call it.''

"It seems they distrust all Outsiders without reason."

"Not without reason," she quickly returned, obeying an impulse to defend her people—for that was how she thought of them. In spite of her having only one-quarter Romany blood, in spite of never having been fully accepted among them and of living the first eight years of her life as any other young English lady had, Artemis Rose still thought of herself as Romany, and she always would. "They are ill-treated everywhere they go. They have been rejected, disparaged, and even hunted down. They have every reason to be wary and distrustful. And yet they took us in when we had nowhere else to go."

"You could have come to Stonechase, I am certain. You would have been welcome here for as long as you wished to stay." He gave a soft smile. "You still are."

A lump formed in her throat. She was certain he meant what he said, but she could hardly settle at Stonechase Manor. Even if she were inclined to accept such generous charity for herself, she still had the baby to consider—a baby of whom Orion and his mother knew nothing. What could Artemis say? *Why thank you, Orion! I would love to impose on your generosity and stay here forever, and oh! by the way, I shall be sending for my baby sister for you to feed, clothe, and educate, as well.* No. It was simply out of the question. Raising Anna was her own responsibility, and that was that.

"Thank you, Orion. You are most kind . . . but I cannot stay."

He didn't press her, and they found the parlor without further conversation.

She troubled her mind no further with thoughts of staying at Stonechase. Optimistic by nature, Artemis believed everything would work out in the end. She always tried to live in the moment, to enjoy what the path set before her, and right then, Artemis was pleased to find she and Orion were evenly matched opponents.

Her father had taught her to play chess the year before he died. Her Romany companions loved the game, and she'd played thousands of matches. She knew she was a good player. She had Orion cornered before too long. She wondered if he realized it. Five moves and she'd have him checkmated, unless he anticipated and acted within the next two moves. She suppressed a happy-puppy wiggle of anticipation. It would feel good to best Orion. She stole a glance at his face. He was studying the board, but he looked completely unconcerned.

*Good.*

Outside, the sky had darkened and the wind had risen. It whistled through the arbor and over the manor's gray stonework as garden flotsam tumbled over the lawn. A few ducks scurried for cover.

Artemis was about to deliver Orion the killing blow when Lady Lindenshire sailed through the door and then hesitated a second before continuing to the bank of windows at the other side of the room, where she began pacing at once and waving her fan agitatedly. Orion and Artemis traded questioning looks and then slid their gazes back to the countess. A few heavy raindrops dashed themselves against the glass, but she paid the gathering storm no heed. Clearly, her attention was focused somewhere else.

"What is the matter, Mama?" Orion finally queried.

She spun about, startled. "What? Oh! Oh . . ." She sighed. "It is hardly worth disturbing your game over. Do continue playing." She began pacing once more.

Orion's brow furrowed. Mama was usually irrepressibly cheerful, so her fretful countenance had him worried. He hated to see her upset over anything, and he was in the habit of shielding her from harm—harm she often brought down upon herself with her stubbornness.

Not that Orion would have her any other way. He

admired his mother and wished there were more ladies like her among the *ton*. She was an independent lady, one who dressed at the height of fashion but who didn't *think* about fashion all the time. One who held a voucher to Almack's but who did not always attend. One who knew who had been present at Carleton House the past evening, but who did not particularly care.

That's the sort of lady Orion wanted for himself, but they were deucedly difficult to come by, and then when one did manage to find oneself a female who could think of something other than fripperies and who did or did not hold vouchers to Almack's, she got snatched from under one's nose by some handsome pirate!

He scowled and then noticed Artemis was giving him a quizzical look. By the devil, he had forgotten completely about the chess game and his mother!

He turned to Artemis, mouthed "Sorry," and silently moved her knight and bishop along with one of his pawns—the very sequence of moves she'd obviously been planning. Then he flicked a glance at his mother, gave Artemis a wink, and exclaimed, "Checkmate? I never saw it coming. Well done! How satisfying to find such a worthy opponent."

"Indeed," Artemis said with a smile. She didn't know which pleased her more: that he had known her strategy all along or that he had sacrificed the game for the comfort of his mother. In spite of his fashionable façade, Artemis liked the man Orion had become.

"I demand a rematch," she said with a sly smile.

He nodded and returned her smile. "You shall have one, I promise. Mama," he said, raising his voice a notch, "the game is over. Come, tell us what troubles you."

The countess rang for tea and the three of them sat upon a pair of elegant sofas. Then the countess leaned close. "Florence has run away."

"Your companion? Where has she gone?"

"She has eloped! With the under gardener. It is all

in here." She waved a crumpled note. "She says they are in love."

"Love," Orion said, "is a delicacy, and most get only the barest taste. If Florence is able to feast, then good for her!"

"Perhaps," the countess conceded. "I do wish her happy, truly I do. But her romantic adventure is dreadfully inconvenient for me. I need her."

Lady Lindenshire, Artemis had learned, was very independent-minded. After the death of her husband, when Orion was only a few weeks old, she had never remarried. She espoused greater freedom and independence for ladies, and she practiced the same whenever she could. Though she was not one to set propriety to nought, she was not averse to bending it a little.

One manifestation of that was that she apparently eschewed the employment of a footman—or any other man—to usher her about Town, delivering packages and calling cards, opening and knocking on doors, and lending propriety. She opted instead for the presence of a female companion. She opened her own doors, and she either had packages delivered or she carried them herself.

"Lady Marlborough has invited me to her grandson's christening. It would be dreadful to miss it. Yet traveling to London alone is not the thing."

Orion shrugged. "You could break tradition for once and use a perfectly normal footman."

"*I?* Break tradition?" his mother cried with a chuckle. "No, I will not use a footman, even if it means missing the christening. I am afraid I shall have to send my regrets."

"Come now, surely Miss Dove will not be that difficult to replace. I daresay there are any number of suitable young ladies—"

"Did you say 'Miss *Dove*'?" Artemis asked, her fingers trembling. Looking from one to the other of them, she set down her cup and saucer with care. "I interpreted the dove I saw as a sign of peace, but that was not it at all. Lady Lindenshire, I—''

"Oh!" the countess blurted. "Why yes . . . of course!" The countess laughed. "The dove! I see."

"See what?" Orion asked.

"Yes." She ignored him. "It is a perfect solution."

"What solution?"

"Do you not see, Orion? *Miss* Dove and *the* dove."

"What dove?" Orion asked. "Who? What?"

The countess looked at Artemis and gave a delicate shrug. "It will come to him in a moment."

"He does not see clearly."

"Never did."

"What am I supposed to be seeing?" Orion asked irritably, unsure of which annoyed him more: that they were making no sense, or that *they* seemed to think they were making perfect sense.

"The signs," the countess answered. "Do you not remember the story of how Artemis came to us? She saw a dove. It was a sign meaning she is destined to take the place of Miss Dove."

"Destined? Really, Mama, you do not truly believe in all that sign nonsense. It is rubbish."

"Then how to explain the dove?"

"Coincidence, and not a very unlikely one at that. The countryside is full of the creatures." A sense of alarm clawed at Orion's sense of calm. "Mama," he said, "please think with your head and not with your heart. Engaging Artemis as your companion will not work."

"Why ever not?" his mother asked.

"You do not know her well enough."

"Piffle! I was present at her birth—and having very early birth pains myself," she said on a nostalgic sigh.

"But she has lived her entire adult life away from here."

"That does not signify. I knew her during the most impressionable time of her life, her first eight years. I liked her then, and I like her now." That pronouncement was accompanied by a stubborn set to his mother's jaw. "I think her becoming my companion is the perfect solution for all of us. Artemis needs a position quite badly—forgive me, my dear—and nothing would please me more than to help the daughter of my dear friend. And you . . ."

"What about me?" Orion asked warily.

His mother dimpled. "Well, dearest, if our Artemis leaves us, whom will you spar with?"

*Our Artemis.* Orion frowned. Mama had certainly taken to Artemis. Too much so. Combine the chit's resemblance to her mother and the fact that she was probably close to Louisa's age the last time his mama saw her, and of *course* his mama had bonded with Artemis— which was irrational, of course. There was no logical reason for the two of them to have formed such a close acquaintance in so short a time. Artemis and Louisa Rose were two different people entirely—but it wouldn't help matters to point that out to his mama. No, there wasn't a blasted thing Orion could do about the connection now.

"I daresay," his mama said, "that our Artemis is the only worthy opponent you have ever encountered here in the country."

Prior to that moment, he'd been delighted with "their" Artemis's cleverness. She'd nearly bested him at chess a few minutes before, which had pleased him no end. So why was the suggestion that her intellect was equal to his so irritating to him now? He didn't know, but if he didn't do or say something right then, he would be stuck with her blasted intellect. As Mama's companion, Artemis would be always underfoot, both here at Stonechase and in Town, where Mama was not unknown to show up at the same functions he did.

He tried to calm down and think rationally. From the moment she'd announced she had no place to go, Orion had known he would have to rescue her, of course, but he'd thought to do so by finding a position for her at one of his estates—preferably the one farthest from London. He'd felt ill at the thought of what might have befallen her had she bypassed Stonechase and proceeded to London on her own.

London would not have been kind to a young lady newly arrived with no employment, no references, and no place to stay. Especially a young lady as pretty as Artemis. Alone on the streets, she'd have ended up in St. Giles or Spitalfields at some flash house or gaming hell. Or in the clutches of a hardened procuress.

Inside, he shuddered. She'd have been eaten alive. He knew he ought to be grateful to his mother for rescuing him from having to rescue Artemis. That wouldn't have been an easy task. The stubborn wench likely would not have accepted an offer of employment from him, and then he would have had to take drastic measures to stop her from hieing off to London alone.

An image of himself forcefully imprisoning her entered his mind.

*Ridiculous.*

An image of himself slipping a wedding ring onto her hand . . .

*Beyond* ridiculous!

Yes, he should be grateful for his mother's intervention, he supposed, but as his mother's companion, Artemis would appear on the periphery of *his* social circle—and she was not the sort of person to remain there blessedly unnoticed and unremarked upon.

He shifted uncomfortably. "Perhaps another position in your household would be more suitable, Mama." *Like a parlor maid, perhaps . . . a milkmaid . . . a seamstress, even.* "She . . . she has nothing suitable to wear as companion."

"She looks very well to me."

Artemis squinted down at her travel-weary skirt and wrinkled her nose. "I believe your son is quite right, Lady Lindenshire. I have little more than what I have on besides a few scarves, a pair of stockings, and another chemise. Such Romany attire is hardly suitable for the companion of a countess."

"There," Orion said. "You see?"

"Piffle!" The countess waved her hand. "I will provide a new wardrobe, of course. You are grasping at straws, Orion. What can you possibly object to?" Her voice hardened, and she put her hand on her hip. "In spite of her unconventional upbringing, Artemis is a pleasant enough young woman, you must agree. She is neither loud nor uneducated nor untrustworthy. I know those traits are often paired with Gypsies—in the minds of the ignorant, that is." She threw him a scathing, challenging look. "*You* are not ignorant, are you, Orion?"

"A week ago," Orion said truthfully, "I was. But no more. If Artemis is any indication, the Gypsies are a civilized people, for she is a lady."

"Come then, what is your true objection to her becoming my companion?"

What *was* his reasoning? Orion did not know. He searched his mind for a rational explanation for his unjustifiable objections but came up with nothing. Artemis, though a Gypsy in her heart and mind, had been all that was amiable and straightforward. In truth, he'd been hoping she would relent and consent to stay with them for a few days. So why did he feel in his bones this dread that she was now set to become his mother's companion?

The only real objection he could come up with was that business with her silly superstitions. He had worked hard to build his reputation among the *ton*. He had become a man of fashion, and he lived at the very pinnacle of society's regard. His rivals would be only too delighted to encourage his mother's companion to display her Gypsy peculiarities.

At his hesitation, his mother waved her hand dismissively and turned to Artemis. "Please, my dear . . .

please tell me your heart is not set on becoming a scullery maid."

Artemis laughed. "I confess it is not!"

Lady Lindenshire laughed, too, and took Artemis's hands in hers, pressing them and beaming. "We shall have such a lovely time choosing your wardrobe, my dear. You will adore my mantua maker. Madame Aneault is a genius, and she will be delighted with you. I am too tall, and she always complains tall is not fashionable, as though it is a choice I have made, but you . . . why, you are a tiny china doll. Madame will enjoy—" Lady Lindenshire went on enthusiastically.

Artemis wished her heart could be as light as the countess's. But in the back of her mind she was worrying over the one wrinkle in the perfect plain of her future: Anna. She knew she couldn't put off explaining about her baby sister any longer. And though she was admittedly unfamiliar with tonnish ways, she was quite sure that hired companions with small children to care for were rare indeed. Rare, as in nonexistent. She wasn't particularly worried, though.

She was well nigh certain the unconventional Lady Lindenshire would allow her to send and care for Anna. Especially after she heard the story of Anna's birth.

And, though it had been impossible *as a guest* to accept Orion's offer to stay on at Stonechase and bring Anna to stay there too, as an *employee* it seemed perfectly natural. The butler had a family. So had the housekeeper, the head groom, the head gardener. Yes, it was quite proper and acceptable for her to bring Anna with her under these new circumstances, but as Artemis opened her mouth to explain about her sister, lightning flashed with an well nigh simultaneous thunderclap. Both ladies yelped, and even Orion started.

The storm had finally broken upon them.

A sudden, blinding wall of gray rain swept across the lawn and lashed viciously against the windows, and with it came a wind that howled over the stonework. A second, double bolt of lightning flashed and boomed from farther away—and Artemis saw that the first bolt had struck a stone birdbath in clear view of the window not twenty paces away on the lawn. The stone cherub that graced the birdbath had been knocked from its pedestal. The little statue had come to rest on the ground, where a pile of wet, windswept leaves had covered it instantly, nearly hiding it from view.

"Goodness!" Lady Lindenshire said. "That was loud enough to knock the thoughts from my head. You, too, by the look." The countess patted Artemis's hand. "Did you wish to say something, my dear?"

Artemis stared at the cherub. "No," she said. "No, there is nothing I wish to say. Nothing at all."

# CHAPTER THREE

Orion looked from his mother to Artemis. Their lovely faces mirrored their eager happiness. Inwardly, he groaned. Nothing would change their minds now. Artemis was his mother's new companion, and that, as Artemis was wont to say, was that.

*Blast!*

Attempting to maintain his status with his disconcertingly eccentric mother a part of the London scene was difficult enough, but with Artemis at her side? He could just see it: they'd all be at some important ball, and Artemis would publicly declare she'd seen a sign— the prince sneezing, perhaps, or Lady Jersey's nose twitching. Good grief! And if she believed in signs, what other Gypsy rubbish did she subscribe to? Would she someday pull a crystal ball from under her skirts?

One thing was certain, such behavior would reflect badly upon him. If her Gypsyish behavior went too far— and how could it not, with his mother to encourage such nonsense?—he'd be a laughingstock.

But then he looked once more at her threadbare clothes, at the boots that looked as though they were full of holes and two sizes too small, and Orion chided himself. What did a little tarnish on his reputation matter if it meant poor Artemis would be settled happily?

She'd had enough ill treatment in her life, and she'd come out of it a fine person. She didn't behave outlandishly. She was well spoken and had pretty manners. Except for her unfortunate preoccupation with portents, she behaved as the lady she was born to be. Perhaps he truly hadn't anything to worry about at all.

Really, he reassured himself, he and his mother ran in very different circles. Everyone in London thought his mama was a bit odd, but since they hardly glimpsed each other above two or three times a season, her influence upon his position in Society, for good or ill, was mitigated. Perhaps he would be but little affected by her companion's misbehavior. Yes, surely Artemis, no matter how outrageously she behaved, could have but little effect upon him.

Just the same, his status within society, as any other narrow apex, was brittle, and he intended to protect it, just in case, by avoiding guilt by association. Artemis was a lady, but he would stay away from that particular lady as much as possible when in Town until he was sure she wasn't going to do anything outrageously Gypsyish. Keeping his distance shouldn't be difficult. In fact, it would be easy. A guinea or two in the palm of his mother's butler would earn him all that good man's intelligence. He'd know which functions to attend and which to avoid. Yes. His mother was right, after all. Artemis's becoming her companion was indeed the best solution for them all.

It was certainly a perfect solution for his mother and for Artemis. A slightly odd companion would suit Lady Lindenshire's independent character, and as for Artemis . . .

His mother broke into his thoughts. "You hesitate, Orion. You have no real objection, do you? I thought not," she said, not waiting for a response. "It is settled, then." She turned to Artemis. "I fancy you and I are two peas in a pod, just as your mother and I were. I am quite certain we shall bump along together very well indeed."

Orion still felt uneasy. "I am certain you will both find your association pleasant," he said and quit the room on the excuse of checking on his horse.

Puzzled, Artemis watched Orion go. He had capitulated too suddenly, and she wondered what had gone on in his mind. "Lady Lindenshire—"

"Belle, Artemis. You must call me Belle."

Artemis smiled. "Belle, I . . . Orion is right. My clothing is—"

"Charming. Your clothing is charming, my dear."

"But," Artemis persisted, knowing the countess was merely being polite, "it is not appropriate for the christening."

Lady Lindenshire waved her hand. "We shall have some things made up for you posthaste."

"Yes, but . . . when *is* the christening?"

"The christening?" the countess repeated, as though hearing the word for the first time. "Oh! I see. Yes, yes, my dear. Bless me, you are quite right. The babe is to be christened eleven days hence, and you," she said with a tip of her delicate head, "must engage Madame Aneault's services as soon as you arrive in London. Madame works miracles, to be sure, but she gets testy if she must perform them in less than a fortnight."

She rang for her portable writing desk. The lovely rosewood box with a hinged and angled top was delivered promptly, and the countess sat scribbling and tapping her narrow quill thoughtfully for a few minutes as Artemis sat down to a cup of strong, sweet, fragrant tea.

"Here now," Lady Lindenshire said at last. "This is a list of the garments and accessories you will require." She blotted the thin, cream-colored paper and handed it over gingerly.

Artemis's eyes goggled. The list was enormous. It began with *fourteen pair fine gauge stockings, white.*

"*Fourteen* pair?" Artemis exclaimed.

"Two per day, my dear. Ladies' feet, contrary to what they might pretend, do perspire."

"*Eight* morning gowns?"

"One for each day of the week, plus an extra for emergencies," Belle explained, as though it was a matter of common sense.

"And another eight dresses just for walking?" Artemis's eyes scanned down the list. "Ball gowns, two riding habits, bonnets, caps, garters, nightrails . . . surely I do not need all this!"

Lady Lindenshire laughed merrily. "Surely you do not question my judgment?"

"No, Belle, of course not, but—"

"But it is my taste you cannot rely upon?"

Artemis gave a roll of her eyes. "You are bamming me."

The countess laughed again. "I certainly am, my dear. Pay no heed to the length of that list. It is not excessive. You are simply unaccustomed to having what you should have had all along." She threw a black look in the direction of Branleigh.

Artemis wondered if Lady Lindenshire's friends would agree.

Artemis did look very like her mother. When she accompanied Lady Lindenshire at society functions, someone was bound to notice the resemblance. Would they be as quick to accept her as Belle had been? As quick to lay blame upon those who had cast Artemis aside?

Artemis was the granddaughter of an earl, but she was also the granddaughter of a Gypsy. She *was* a Gypsy now. Artemis knew that didn't matter to the countess, but would it matter to her friends?

* * *

The storm had brought with it a heavy chill, and it seemed it might snow as the pair of lumbering coaches and the baggage cart hastened to London. The Stone-chase maids she traveled with kept up a steady stream of chatter during the ten-hour trip, and Artemis joined in, except when they neared London, when she couldn't resist staring out the window.

She'd been to Bristol once, and she'd thought that city enormous, but this! She'd been wrong about Bristol. It was but a village compared to London. The streets were crowded with every type of equipage, from the most elegant barouches to the lowliest gigs and traps, from the fastest phaetons to the lumbering merchant wagons.

And the noise! Drivers of mail coaches, hacks, and delivery wagons hailed each other as they passed. The clip-clopping of the horses' hooves and the jingling of their traces, the rolling and creaking. The loud calls of the baker and the pie man and their heated haggling with their customers. Shrieks of children playing, dogs barking, water splashing from an upstairs window to the street below. Church bells, cow bells, ox bells, mongers' bells, and ships' bells out on the Thames. Artemis had never heard such a cacophony.

And then, almost as though someone had covered her ears and eyes with something thick and woolly, the noise and crush abated, and the coaches rolled onto a quiet and shady street lined with stately chestnut trees. Buildings of plaster and wood gave way to stone, which in turn gave way to marble as the procession entered a large square with a green park in the center and enormous houses all round.

Lady Lindenshire's fine, tall house was situated on a corner, and as they approached, the maids gathered their shawls and tied their white cap strings, making ready to disembark. Yet no sooner had the coaches stopped than a cry of dismay rose into the chill morning air. A maid had emerged from the house, smudged from head to toe in black.

There had been a fire that very morning, it seemed, a largish one, the result of an overturned lamp. The damage to the drawing room was not great, but much of the first floor of the house was coated in a greasy soot. This was very unwelcome news to the poor maids from Stonechase Manor, and Artemis felt sorry for them.

"Soot like that is terrible hard to clean off," one remarked to Artemis, "and smoke goes everywhere. We'll have to polish every last inch of that house."

"I shall be glad to help."

"Oh, miss, you're a right 'un, and no mistake." The maid smiled gratefully.

They all alighted, and Artemis was following the housekeeper inside when the butler stopped her. Peabody was a trusted servant, and he evidently traveled to oversee the servants wherever Lady Lindenshire was in residence. Artemis imagined he could be an imposing figure, tall and broad-shouldered as he was, gray at the temples, and full of dour authority, though she found his countenance kindly enough as he addressed her now.

"Miss Artemis," he began, using the name she'd been called as a child. Miss Rose would be have been the proper form of address, since she was an eldest—and, indeed, only—daughter. But, with "Master Orion" running about, she supposed no one had been able to resist pairing the two names, linked as they were in mythology, so "Miss Artemis" it had always been and still was. "The house is in disarray," Peabody continued, "a sooty pot of chaos. It is no place for a lady. Might I suggest you—"

"Oh, but I am not a lady, I am companion to—"

"You were born a lady," he said with an imperious sniff. "Lady Lindenshire will treat you as such, and so will I."

Artemis gave a warm but sheepish smile. "Thank you."

"Might I suggest you repair to Master Orion's small town house for a day or two?"

"Without Orion's invitation?" she asked doubtfully.

"Miss Artemis, Lady Lindenshire made it clear to the servants that she regards you more as a dear family friend than as another servant—and dear friends do *not* require formal invitations, especially when their need is urgent, as it is now."

"Yes, yes. I see your point. But, in truth, Mr. Peabody, my situation is unique. I am not simply a family friend, and I really ought to stay. You shall need every available pair of hands to help clean the soot away, and—what?"

The poor man had gone quite red in the face. "Miss Artemis, either you are a guest, or you are a servant. If you are a guest, then you must stay elsewhere."

Artemis dimpled. "Then I am not a guest," she said and stepped past him.

"*However,*" he said loudly at her back, and Artemis stopped, "if you are a servant, then you must follow my orders, and I will forbid you to do any work at all. You will stay here, and two maids will attend you instead of helping with the repairs—a state of affairs that will only create more work for the others, not less."

"Check and mate," Artemis returned.

"I know," the butler said with a wink and a smile. Then he bowed low. "My lady, it will be our pleasure to serve a guest such as you."

She gave a wry smile. "You, Mr. Peabody, are a piece of work."

"Why, thank you, Miss Artemis!" He looked genuinely pleased.

Artemis agreed to remove herself to Orion's house. Staying there could do no harm. After all, she would be still be well chaperoned by his servants, and Orion was not in Town, anyway.

Which was why, when a certain gentleman happened

to pass through Silver Street late the next morning, the unexpected activity at the Earl of Lindenshire's small town house captured his attention, and why, when said gentleman decided to pay an impromptu call, he found a raven-haired beauty presiding over Orion's parlor.

*Sans* Orion.

# CHAPTER FOUR

George DeMoray, the Viscount Whitemount, was surprised, to say the least. The lady—the footman addressed her as "Miss Artemis"—received him in the parlor with a frank, almost eager smile. Her eyes matched almost exactly the icy blue of the draperies, but her manner was warm. George was amazed. He hadn't heard the first whisper of news concerning the impending arrival of guests at Lindenshire's town house.

If he was astonished to find a lady presiding over Lindenshire's parlor, he was positively flummoxed over her garments, for they were clearly Gypsy. It was much too early to be dressing for a masquerade—and it was unheard of to receive guests dressed that way. Upon no more than two seconds' reflection, however, George was glad she had. Though clothed in little more than silk scarves and coarse black cloth, she was breathtakingly attractive. She was not classically beautiful. She did not possess the golden ringlets, plump figure, or wide-set eyes that were the thing those days, but her alabaster skin cut a striking contrast with her raven-dark tresses, and the scarves of blue and green she wore clung to her slight, yet still curvaceous, figure in a most alluring fashion. Orion's parlor had never held such interest!

Or such a crowd.

The lady was surrounded by three dressmakers, two milliners, and a shoemaker. Several dozen open boxes lay strewn at her feet, and costly fabric and laces, which she'd obviously been in process of choosing, were draped over her lap and the arms of her chair, so that she appeared to be floating in a sea of red silk, gold brocade, snowy muslin, and deep blue satin. Her skin wasn't much darker than the white lace she held. It was creamy-white and unblemished.

She rose to greet him, and George's sensitive nose detected a faint wafting of sandalwood. The exotic fragrance matched her countenance. She had lovely black hair that hung in curls down her back, the bluest eyes, and the thickest eyelashes George had ever seen. She almost *looked* like a Gypsy, by Jove!

But her melodious and cultured voice put that notion to rest. This was no Gypsy maid, but a lady. Who was she, this Artemis? George had never seen her, of that he was certain. He'd never even heard of her.

Perhaps Artemis was not her true name. The thought occurred to George suddenly. Perhaps she wasn't what she seemed—which seemed plausible enough, dressed as she was.

As she dismissed her attendants, it was painfully obvious she wasn't used to directing servants—or anyone else. Why, even as she sent the frippery-sellers off to the kitchen for a nibble and sup, she apologized for inconveniencing them!

"Where are my manners?" she said, turning to George. "I am afraid I have been at caravan too long. Would you care for some refreshment? Tea, perhaps? I should not have dismissed the servants without asking. Now I shall have to pull the bell. My addled brain will have added extra steps to their sore feet."

George's mouth was hanging open as she motioned for him to sit down, patting the arm of the sofa beside her.

Caravan? Had she truly just said *caravan?*

George clapped his trap shut and accepted her offer of tea. She was a Gypsy, by Jove! Her lovely mouth had just confirmed what her manner, her dress, and her coloring had already declared. It was as plain as the huge diamond pin in George's cravat. She was a Gypsy. A Gypsy! And yet she spoke with perfect diction and elegant tone.

An elegant Gypsy?

The combination was . . . most intriguing.

She rang for tea, turned back to him, and smiled openly. "So, you are a friend of Orion's?"

*Orion!* He blinked at the easy familiarity with which Lindenshire's given name spilled from the young woman's red lips. Where did she fit into Lindenshire's life? Or, more to the point, where did Lindenshire fit into hers?

Who was she? Surely not a servant, he thought, eyeing the costly fabrics she'd been perusing as he'd arrived. A fiancée? Nonsense! Orion Chase, the toplofty Earl of Lindenshire, connect himself with a Gypsy? Never.

A cousin, perhaps? Yes, that had to be it. A cousin. A married cousin, he amended, since there wasn't a duenna, a mama, or even a bored servant in sight. Even with the parlor doors left wide open as they were, only a married lady would receive him thus, alone and unaccompanied.

George's eyes had gone unfocused. The Gypsy brought him back from the ether with the wave of one slender white hand in front of his nose. "Pardon me!" he blurted. "What were you saying? Am I a friend of Orion's? Yes, yes. Well . . . the Earl of Lindenshire and I . . . enjoy a long acquaintance. We met long ago at Eton. He was head boy, at the top of our class, and I was second." *And nothing has changed,* he added to himself as he waited for the lady to reciprocate within the confines of the conversation and reveal her connection to the Earl of Lindenshire. When the seconds stretched awkwardly and it became clear no such explanation was forthcoming, he said, "I am at your service, my lady." He bowed over her hand. "I gather . . . Lindenshire is not currently at home?"

"I am afraid not. Orion is in the country, and I do not know when to expect him here in town. Perhaps not for several weeks."

Whoever-she-was was installed here in Orion's town house without him for weeks? She had to be family. A Gypsy in Orion's family? Delicious! "So you and Orion are . . . cousins?" he probed.

"No, we are not related. I have known Orion for a long time. We are . . . good friends."

Not related? "And your husband is?" George fished.

"Nonexistent." She dimpled. "I am not married."

Another possible explanation popped into George's mind, and he well nigh gasped. Could it be she was *one of those?*

A maid arrived with tea, and he used the time to plan what to say next. The manner in which she received—or parried—a carefully constructed compliment would tell him what he wanted to know. "I do not collect how Lindenshire can stay away, not with such beauty awaiting him." His arms gestured about the room, but he kept his gaze trained upon Artemis, and he kept it as warm as possible.

She neither blushed nor dropped her gaze, but looked him straight in the eye and said, "London holds precious little fascination for him, I believe."

"Ah, now that I cannot believe. You are a beautiful young lady, and therefore you must have secured his fascination."

A smile twitched about her rosy lips. "Orion does not appreciate my particular talents. Truth to tell, he does not know I am here, but if he did, I am certain he would not come dashing to London. In fact, I am sure I would not be entirely welcome here.''

Of that the viscount was certain, and it took a herculean effort to stop the grin that tried to slide onto his face. Yes, Orion Chase would likely suffer an apoplexy if he discovered his Gypsy mistress presiding over his very fashionable town house—for that was what she was, the viscount was now certain. He should have realized it as soon as he heard her name. Artemis, indeed! What other name would Orion's mistress take? Orion, the hunter who pursues and catches the Goddess of the Hunt!

And if that false name were not enough evidence, here she was spending what promised to be an enormous pile of Orion's blunt, surrounded as she was in a sea of exquisite materials and attended by London's most exclusive mantua maker. "Miss Artemis" was Orion's mistress.

His Gypsy mistress.

His *secret* Gypsy mistress—and the fashionable Earl of Lindenshire no doubt wished to keep her so—which placed George at a very interesting crossroads, for now *he* knew Orion's secret.

Orion Chase was the viscount's fiercest social rival. He was planted firmly at the very peak of Society's regard, the crème de la crème, which irritated George no end. Throughout their boyhoods, Lindenshire had been a nothing. Bookish and scrawny, he hadn't been a threat to George except in academics, which George didn't give a fig for anyway.

But then, two years ago, Lindenshire had begun to dress more fashionably and to attend a few balls here or there. Still, he had hovered on the periphery of the *ton's* notice until three months ago, when he'd suddenly burst forth from obscurity and captured the attention of London Society, usurping George's place in the process. To George's unending irritation, Lindenshire had become the pinkest pink of the *ton*.

Like George, Lindenshire dressed in the first stare of fashion and attended all the best functions. They were both respectably muscular, dashingly handsome, and deliriously wealthy. They were both admired, emulated, and envied wherever they went. But each time they found themselves in the same room, it was Lindenshire people craned their necks to see. Lindenshire they admired. Lindenshire they talked about the next morning.

Only after Lindenshire came into the scene did anyone discover the amusing way "Viscount Whitemount" rhymed. He was certain that, in spite of his wealth and his dashing countenance, the thought of becoming the "Viscountess Whitemountess" would give any young lady pause. That deuced devil Lindenshire was at the top of every matchmaking mama's list, while George was . . . second fiddle. Day-old bread. Tarnished gold. And he was tired of it.

As the Gypsy rang for tea, his gaze swept her lithe form appreciatively. She moved just as she spoke, with a sort of graceful frankness. No mincing steps or simpering words for her.

She was unusual, alluring, exotic.

And she belonged to Orion Chase.

But not for long. Not if George had anything to do with it.

If he could steal this beauty from Orion, seduce her right away from Lindenshire's own town house in his absence, Orion would be the object of much amused conversation. And George would take his place at the top.

As they chatted about the weather, half of George's mind was busy wondering if he *could* seduce her. His confidence was not as robust as he would like, but that was no matter, he supposed, for he didn't actually have to seduce her away from Orion. No, it would be enough just to *appear* to have seduced her. And a certain ball *was* approaching. . . .

George pasted an expression of alarm upon his face and stilled, his teacup halfway to his mouth. "Oh, dear!"

"My lord?"

"You say Orion will be away some days yet?"

She nodded. "Weeks, most likely. Why? What is amiss?"

"Then you have no escort for the ball?"

"What ball?"

"What ball? My dear, you have been kept tucked away in the country, have you not? Hmmph." He hoped he sounded properly indignant upon her behalf. "To be sure, it is not the grandest ball he could attend with you, but it is the only one this time of year. Were he here, he would surely escort you there."

"Indeed not, sir, for I am little more than a servant, and I am not even supposed to be here." She gestured about her at the sparingly furnished but elegant little parlor.

George blinked. Had he heard her properly? Had this pretty little bird been made to feel she was a mere servant? Suddenly, he took note of her lack of diamond trinkets. He didn't know a man who wasn't obliged to gift his mistress a sparkler now and then. Sparklers they displayed as a general displays his medals, hard won in battle. But as far as George could tell, this female hadn't so much as a golden earring.

Well, well . . . his chances were improving. Orion's inattentiveness would make George's task only easier.

"You are not a servant, my dear. Anyone can see that."

She looked confused. "They can?"

"Certainly!" The viscount tried to appear scandalized. "Yes, and it would be a great insult not to attend the ball."

"You mean that if Orion does not attend—"

"Exactly. It would be seen as an insult. A social slap to the face. Could harm one's very reputation, ruin your chances . . . elsewhere, if you know what I mean."

"But . . . but he is not even in London. Neither is Lady Lindenshire. No one is. And I am not supposed to be here in his house."

"Ah, but you *are* here," he said, "and people—such as myself!—have taken notice. It would be a great slight to one's reputation not to attend."

"Oh, dear. Poor Orion!"

George nearly fainted at the young woman's naïveté, but somehow he hung on long enough to suggest a way out of her pickle.

# CHAPTER FIVE

As Artemis, on the Viscount Whitemount's arm, approached the ornate doors of an otherwise nondescript house the next evening, she hoped for the thousandth time she was doing the right thing. She'd looked for a sign, of course, but she hadn't seen anything to reassure her. She simply had to rely upon the viscount's judgment, for, in spite of her birth and first eight years as a properly brought up young lady, she was quite out of her element where tonnish ways were concerned. The life of a Gypsy did not require one to pay close attention to the doings of the fashionable world. She was hopelessly ignorant, while, clearly, the viscount was not. Artemis was very grateful to have him to guide her through this peril.

She nervously smoothed her gown as they stepped over the threshold. Madame Aneault truly could work miracles, it seemed. She had delivered the gown in person an hour ago and performed the final adjustments to it herself. Artemis cringed at the extra cost the speed incurred, but it could not have been helped.

As they stepped down onto a wide, polished wood floor, a liveried footman announced their arrival:

"The Viscount Whitemount," he said in a nasally voice, "and Artemis."

Her heart gave three beats before she realized the footman was not going to announce her surname. She threw Whitemount a questioning look, which he returned. *My name?* she mouthed.

His mouth formed an *O* and he nodded. "You were announced as Artemis. Do you wish to change that?"

She nodded. She didn't fancy there could be many Artemises in London, but since she was the Lindenshires' only representative at this important function, she didn't want there to be any mistake. She wanted everyone to know exactly which Artemis was in attendance; she wanted the footman to announce her as Artemis Rose.

But it was not to be, for the viscount merely patted her hand and said, cryptically, "I am pleased you have decided to change your name, my dear. We will think of something suitable . . . together." Then, before she could make any sense of what he'd said, he pulled her toward a small knot of people clustered around what appeared to be a dais—their host and hostess, she assumed, and her heart fluttered. She'd just have to sort out the viscount's remark about her name later.

As they waited their turn to be recognized, Artemis looked about the room, which when empty, she supposed, would look rather drab. Tonight, however, the room was ablaze with color and light. Gowns of deep, flaming orange or bright spring green competed with buttercup yellow and bluebell purples, while diamonds flashed upon every feminine wrist, neck, and ear.

They were next in line, and the viscount drew her up onto the dais beside him. As she glanced out over the assembly, the sea of vivid color reminded Artemis of a meadow of summer flowers—and her heart sank, for she knew she was hopelessly out of fashion.

The dress Madame Aneault had created for her was of palest blue silk with sky-blue ribbon rosettes scattered about the neckline. When she'd taken the dress out of its box and put it on, she'd been dismayed at how low the neckline was, but she'd reasoned that if that were the fashion, she would simply have to bear it—or bare it, she'd thought wryly. But she needn't have worried. Looking out over the jiggling, heaving, voluminous display of bosoms there at the ball, she could see her own décolletage was modest in comparison—modest and completely out of fashion. The neckline was too high, the color too pale. Even the string of small pearls she wore—an extravagance she had protested back at Stonechase Manor but which Lady Lindenshire seemed to think necessary—set fashion at nought, for they seemed to be the only pearls in the room.

She knew she stuck out like a . . . like a Gypsy at a fancy *ton* ball.

And there was nothing she could do about it. She could not turn tail and depart, for, as the viscount said, people had taken notice of her presence at Orion's town house. It was apparently no matter that she was a hired companion. The viscount said she was not viewed as a servant and it would be a terrible insult if she did not attend the ball.

She knew Orion's reputation as a man of fashion was important to him. The last thing he would wish to do would be to insult the host and hostess of an important ball. Perhaps the insult would go even deeper than that. Perhaps there were important guests there among the crowd—maybe even the prince!—and, for all Artemis knew, it might be seen as an insult to the prince if she left so soon. Though she suspected Lady Lindenshire wouldn't give a fig whom she offended if they were not personal friends of hers, Artemis knew Orion would care very much.

And then the answer came to her: Lady Lindenshire liked to please herself. Artemis suspected she actually

took delight in shocking others. Dressing in the *last*
stare of fashion must be one of her quirks. Her mantua
maker probably dressed her in the same colorless way
as Artemis herself was dressed now. The entire *ton* must
be aware of it. No one was staring at Artemis, which
meant her appearance would have no ill effect upon
Orion's status. So she relaxed and turned to her hostess
with a smile.

But her smile faded fast, like the stars at sunrise.
Instead of the gracious and beautiful woman of her
imagination, their hostess was an ugly crone whose
piercing gaze flicked boldly from Artemis to Whitemount before it returned to make an assessing sweep
from the top of Artemis's head to the toes of her slippers.

"Ah, yes . . . Whitemount's new lady."

Artemis felt her jaw drop. She quickly closed it and
looked to the viscount for his denial, but Whitemount
only tucked her hand more firmly in his arm and smiled,
a smug, self-assured expression Artemis recognized as
pride. Outrage swept through Artemis like a summer
fury. To be sure, she lacked knowledge of the ways of
polite society, and she was unaware of the nuances of
tonnish behavior, but she was quite certain she had
done nothing to lead Lord Whitemount to believe that
she was *his lady*—and she was even more certain he had
done nothing to win her. Yet his refusal to correct their
hostess's spoken assumption, which had seemed to
Artemis quite rash and even rude, could be viewed as
a confirmation. And he knew it!

Artemis pulled her hand from his grasp and curtsied
to their hostess. "Madam. I am Artemis—"

"I know. Everyone knows."

So it was as Whitemount had said. Everyone in Town
knew who she was. The lady was staring at her intensely,
almost as though she expected Artemis to say something
more. "I . . . I offer you Lord and Lady Lindenshire's
regrets, Madam."

The old woman gave a startling bark of laughter and

addressed the viscount. "Oho! You've got yourself a wit there, ain't you, Whitemount?"

Artemis protested, "No, ma'am! You are mistaken, for Lord Whitemount and I are not . . . we do not share any sort of understanding." The viscount looked horrified, but she trudged on. "His Lordship merely offered to escort me to this ball because Lord Lindenshire was unavailable." She turned to the viscount. "Why on earth would you let this good woman assume we—" She stopped. Furious though she was, this was neither the time nor the place to air her grievances with the viscount. She turned back to their hostess. "It . . . it is a lovely room," she said. "Thank you for inviting Lord and Lady Lindenshire."

Artemis gave another small curtsy and moved away. Behind her, the crone remarked to Whitemount, "She thinks I invited Lindenshire's mother?"

"She has been kept in the country and knows well nigh nothing."

"Well, she apparently knows enough to keep Lindenshire happy. Someone ought to educate her on the rest."

"I am doing my best."

"Oho, Whitemount, of that I am certain." She laughed loudly, and as Artemis was wondering how a lady of such ill manners enjoyed such a lofty place in society, she realized she didn't even know the woman's name. They hadn't been properly introduced.

Though she reminded herself that she was not educated on the finer points of proper behavior, it still struck her as odd that the viscount had not introduced her. *Oh, dear!* Perhaps it had never entered his mind that she *wouldn't* know the woman's name. Perhaps everyone knew her name—everyone except Artemis. Who was she? For all Artemis knew, she could be Queen Charlotte!

But Artemis had little time to ponder that problem before another confronted her. A set was forming, and

Whitemount was leading her onto the floor. Before she knew it, there she was. She froze.

"What is the matter?" Whitemount asked.

"I . . . I am afraid I do not know the steps," she said with a blush. Back in caravan, she had been considered quite adept, but here . . .

The viscount goggled at her. "Good heavens, did he never even dance with you?"

"Who?"

"Lindenshire."

"The devil you say!" a tall, balding man cried, before Artemis could reply. "She is Lindenshire's?"

The viscount smiled. "No. Not anymore."

"Yours then?"

"No!" Artemis said, very much annoyed at the assumptions the two were flinging about like feed for the birds to peck. "I do not *belong* to Lindenshire or to Whitemount. I am no man's property. And I would very much appreciate it if you would direct your questions to me—after we have been properly introduced."

The tall man grinned widely and looked to Whitemount. "I see."

She allowed the viscount to lead her to the room's perimeter, where they sat out the dance. But no sooner had the next set begun to form than did a third young man pull her to her feet. "I cannot let so fair a flower wilt alone."

"Sir! I do not know the steps."

"I will teach you, then. Come!" And he did. But not well.

Soon, Artemis was blundering through the steps, forgetting when to step to the side and when to advance and when to circle round. But no one seemed to mind, most certainly not the regiment of other men, young and old, who suddenly converged and seemed to have nothing better to do than to allow Artemis to step on their toes. It was all very odd.

The rest of the ball was just as odd. Artemis suddenly felt everyone was staring at her, and the viscount stuck to her like pitch. She'd thought she would enjoy the event, but she could not. Everyone seemed to know each other, as no introductions were made, even to her. The dancers were a little too ... free with their movements, and the conversationalists a little too loud and free with their gossip. She even overheard several bawdy puns—and so did some other ladies, judging by their gay trills of laughter.

It was the same sort of behavior she'd heard Gypsies accused of, over and over, and it was all keenly unsettling. Not at all what she had expected.

Her first eight years spent at Branleigh had led her to expect society functions to be much more staid. In fact, as the night wore on, she began to suspect that the viscount—and Orion—moved in rather *fast* circles. The evidence was all about her. For one thing, there were no chaperones. Not a single duenna, mama, or watchful spinster in sight.

It certainly was not what she expected, but then she hadn't really known what to expect, had she? Still, she felt out of place, somehow, and was almost glad when she twisted her ankle and stumbled to the floor, for it gave her an excuse to ask Whitemount to convey her home well before midnight.

The ride home was no less uncomfortable than the ball had been, however, for Whitemount insisted on examining her ankle to ascertain if there were any lasting damage. After pulling off her slipper and manipulating her toes, her arch, and her heel, he pronounced them sound, but then he seemed concerned there might be some damage to her leg bone, as well. His look of concern seemed genuine, but ...

Artemis pulled her foot away. "I am unhurt, truly."

He frowned.

Nothing made sense.

* * *

It wasn't until the next day around midmorning that everything came into focus.

Understanding arrived in the form of a long, velvet lined box delivered to her doorstep—or, rather, the Earl of Lindenshire's doorstep. A footman delivered it along with a card belonging to one Baron Montescue.

Artemis was in the morning parlor writing a letter to Isabel, the woman she'd left chiefly in charge of Anna, when the package arrived. The footman withdrew, and Artemis was very glad he had, for she gave a little scream when she saw the contents of the box.

Pure fire—a double strand of diamonds.

The bracelet slid sinuously from the box and onto her lap, followed by a note, which proved even more astonishing than the diamonds:

> *Dear Lady, Flame of my Heart,*
>
> *The fire in your lovely eyes has burned into my soul. Our dance last night was the most exciting encounter I have ever had. The expressive way you touched me makes me tremble even now.*
>
> *I cannot live without you. I must have you. Say you will be mine, and anything in my power to bestow shall be yours. You have only to utter its name. In the meantime, please accept this gift as a mere token of my sincerity.*
>
> *Awaiting your response, I am,*
> *Devotedly yours,*
> *M*

Artemis ransacked her memory for a face to go along with the name "Montescue." But she had danced with so many gentlemen it had been impossible to keep them all sorted out. She vaguely remembered the name, but . . . but she certainly had not favored him—or any other gentleman—with any such "expressive" touch. Certainly nothing beyond that which was strictly proper within the confines of the dance.

Obviously, however, this Lord Montescue felt differently. "What have I done?" she murmured. She'd been a fool to attend the ball without Lady Lindenshire to school her on the finer points. Curse her Gypsy failings! She must have done something improper. But what? And how was she going to gracefully decline his offer of marriage?

Her trembling fingers stilled. Dear Lord, with Anna to consider, how could she even *think* of turning down an offer of marriage from a titled and most likely very wealthy gentleman? The answer came to her immediately: she couldn't. She had no logical reason to spurn such an offer.

Logic? Orion would be proud.

Which gentleman was Lord Montescue? The older, silver-haired man who had blundered onto her toes, perhaps? Or the red-haired dandy who had made frequent and conspicuous use of a bejeweled quizzing glass? She shook her head, unable to imagine herself as the wife of either one of those gentlemen. She was glad that by sheer numbers it was unlikely either of them were Baron Montescue.

And yet she could not feel any relief, for *one* of the nameless men at the ball did wish to marry her. Whoever he was, he must be terribly shy. Proposals were usually conducted in person, weren't they? And with a ring, rather than a bracelet.

Perhaps, like Lady Lindenshire, Montescue was rather more unconventional than shy. She gave a mirthless bark of laughter. "Ten ducks in a row!" she said, "of course he is unconventional! He wants to marry *me*, does he not?" How much more unconventional could it be for a lord to propose marriage to a lady with no reputation to speak of? With whom he had only the barest of acquaintances? What sort of man was he, this Lord Montescue? "Lord Montescue," she murmured, moving to stare out the tall window. "I do not even remember his face!"

The footman knocked discreetly upon the open parlor door and entered, carrying his silver salver.

Artemis turned and stared.

"For you, miss."

"Another box?" She took it. It seemed to take the footman an eon to remove himself, but finally she was alone and opened the box. More diamonds. This time a necklace. And another note—a love note from the besotted baron, she supposed. She vacillated between wanting to read it and dreading it. *How different it would be were I in love with the sender.* "Or even knew what he looked like," she muttered, unfolding the missive.

She gasped.

The hand was sweeping, extravagant, and it used green ink. Montescue's hand was small, tidy, and black. Her eyes flew across the page:

> *My Dear,*
>
> *After our dance last night, I could not sleep. The promise in your eyes was enough to turn my Soul from dreams. You are the most exquisite lady I have ever seen, as different from all others as the stars are from the sea and just as lofty in my aspiration. I will not rest until you agree to be mine and I have ascended to reside with you among the heavens.*
>
> *Please accept these paltry diamonds, though they be only a dim reflection of your starry beauty. Had you not already the brightest of the stars in your eyes, I would give those to you as well. I beg you will accept me, and I shall ever remain*
>
> > *Hopefully yours,*
> > *A*

*A?*

She looked more closely at the calling card, which

she'd assumed at first to be another from Montescue. "Sir Augustus Vance," she read. *Two* proposals?

Two proposals from two different men? Two proposals accompanied by diamonds, not rings? Two proposals via note, not in person?

Two notes purposely left unsigned!

The footman knocked upon the door a third time, placed a tray on the side table, and withdrew. Upon the tray lay a card, an envelope, and a third box.

Not a ring box.

Artemis sank to a seat next to the fire, the diamond bracelet and necklace dangling from her shaking fingers, the notes forgotten in her hands.

They didn't want to marry her. No, they all thought she was a mistress looking for a protector!

"Even worse," she murmured, "they must all think I am *Orion's* mistress."

# CHAPTER SIX

Blindly, she stumbled to her bedchamber and threw herself onto the four-poster. They didn't want her hand in marriage; they wanted her body in their beds. And why shouldn't they assume she might be agreeable? She had attended a cyprians' ball—for she now realized that was exactly what the ball had been.

She replayed in her mind her words to Lord Whitemount: *I have known Orion for a long time. We are . . . good friends,* she'd said. Finding her residing alone in Orion's town house and ordering gowns from an exclusive mantua maker, of course Whitemount had assumed the worst. *Lindenshire does not appreciate my particular talents,* she'd told him. Well, no wonder the viscount had been so forward! He, along with the others, wished to secure her favors for himself!

A knock sounded upon her chamber door.

"Come," she called.

A maid entered with two more small boxes. She avoided Artemis's eyes and left too quickly.

Did *everyone* know?

She bit her lip and thought about the five men who

were vying for her. Five! Were mistresses that difficult to come by? Why did they want her? Was she such a prize that no man could resist her? Orion's favorite word came to mind. Rubbish! She wasn't ugly, exactly, but she was hardly beautiful enough to inspire such . . . heated devotion. It was a mystery.

She couldn't resist opening the other three boxes, though of course she would have to send them back. Two more bracelets and a brooch, all diamonds. She laughed mirthlessly, remembering the lack of any colored stones at last night's ball. "Of course they are all diamonds! With what else does a man gift his mistress?"

She looked about her bleakly at the lovely room with its delicate furniture and its lovely blue curtains and counterpane. It even had a connecting door to another, smaller room she supposed should have been for a lady's maid. Such a room would be perfect for Anna, and Artemis had hoped Lady Lindenshire's town house would have one something like it. Artemis had planned to ask the countess as soon as the lady arrived in London.

But it didn't matter now. She wouldn't be asking anything of Lady Lindenshire ever again. Artemis could not serve as Lady Lindenshire's companion with all of London believing her to be Orion's mistress—or former mistress. She couldn't even ask the countess for a reference.

She knew better than to hope the scandal would evaporate if she simply explained the misunderstanding publicly. No one would believe her. Not even if Orion and Lady Lindenshire both defended her story. Artemis was wise enough where human nature was concerned to know there would still be those who would prefer to believe the worst.

And, while she might still move about in society were she a titled lady, a Gypsy maid enjoyed no such margin of tolerance among the *ton*. No one would employ her now. Even a position as scullery maid, the lowest of the low, was out of her reach.

She wept.

She had no choice but to leave London. Trying to discover a silver lining, she thought of the city's crushing swirl of smoke and thick, blanketing fog, of the mudlarks, mongers, and urchins, of the human voices raised over the noise of the horses, wagons, and bells. The din never ceased.

In reality, she was lucky. London was no place to rear Anna anyway. Not by herself. She would leave forthwith. Go back to caravan and . . . and—what? Returning to the Gypsies permanently was unthinkable. The caravan was in constant danger, never knowing if they would be welcomed or driven away. The wagon she slept in had several bullet holes in its sides. As a child, she used to look through them to try to wish upon the stars.

She shook herself. Anna had to have better.

And it was up to Artemis to provide it any way she could. But where could she take Anna? Where was she to find work? She wouldn't be able to find a position in any country house of worth. The scandal would follow her eventually. She and Anna would be tossed out into the weather, and what then? Better not even to try for a grand house. No, the best employment she could expect was as tavern maid, and—dear heavens!—she'd be on the edge of starvation even without Anna to care for. How were they to live?

Abruptly, she faced the thought that had inevitably occurred to her as soon as she'd read the second note, the thought she'd pushed aside, the one she'd buried, tried to forget.

She could become a mistress.

She thought of the viscount's hands upon her leg and shuddered. A heavy tear dropped onto the pillow just as she heard the sound of a carriage in the street below.

Moments later, the maid knocked softly on her door once more and entered. "Baron Montescue has arrived, miss, and he desires to know if you are at home."

A lump formed in Artemis's throat. She was not prepared to receive him. She had not determined what she should say to him—or to any other gentlemen who might come calling that day. Accepting any of them was unthinkable. And yet . . . she shook her head. "I will not be receiving visitors today, Megan. Tell him . . . tell him I am suffering from a megrim"—which wasn't untruthful—"and that I cannot—that I regret—no! Just say I am sleeping."

"Yes, miss."

"And . . . if any more packages arrive, pray simply leave them outside my door. I really do wish to sleep."

The maid gave her a kind, understanding smile. "Yes, miss. Will you be taking meals up here, then?"

Artemis wasn't sure she could eat anything at all, but she nodded, and the maid left. The sound of Montescue's carriage rolling away followed soon after. Artemis didn't even go to the window to see what he looked like. All she wanted to do was escape into sleep.

She closed her eyes and cast about for something pleasant to think of, but the only thing that came to mind was Orion. She kept imagining him atop the ruins back at Stonechase Manor. But instead of his usual teasing, cocksure display of laughing brown eyes she loved so well, the dream Orion wore an expression of disapproval. Disapproval and hurt.

The thought of facing him after becoming some man's mistress twisted her heart. What would she say to him? What would he say to her? Not that she need worry about that, she realized, for in all likelihood they would never come face to face again. She would never be welcome anywhere in polite society.

And neither would Anna.

And yet, if she simply stayed in London as Lady Lindenshire's companion, nothing would change. She was certain that, if she asked them, both Orion and Lady Lindenshire would insist she stay—Lady Lindenshire because of her inherent unconventionality and Orion because he was, ultimately, a gentleman. No doubt he would insist there was no scandal, to his utter detriment. But she couldn't stay even at their insistence, for everyone would still believe poor Anna was Orion's child. The scandal would always follow her. She would always be on the edge of the circle, never within.

The choices were all bad.

She wept with silent grief before falling asleep at last and tossing fitfully as the shadows slanted lower and lower and with them the sun's rays. Sunlight crept over the dressing table until it found the diamonds, which glittered fiercely, stabbing bright rainbows into her eyes ... Artemis awakened with a start. As her eyes focused and fixed on the diamonds, the solution to her problem coalesced and resolved along with the view.

She would take the jewelry. Take it and flee London forthwith.

"Stars and signs!" she murmured. That was the answer! She would head for Cornwall, retrieve Anna, and sail for America as soon as she could. They would start a new life there. If she changed her name, the scandal could never touch her or Anna again.

The thought of no longer being Artemis brought with it a sudden pang of—what? Emptiness. Orion in the world without an Artemis. She hadn't seen him for sixteen years, hadn't expected to ever see him again ... and yet she'd always known he was out there, the other half of a pair. Changing her name seemed ... well, unnatural, somehow, like trying to separate sea from strand. Sea and strand, separate yet inseparable, just like she and Orion.

"Rubbish," she said, scowling. As a young girl she had hoped, dreamed that maybe ... maybe she and Orion might meet again. She shook her head. It would do no good to dwell on those childhood fantasies. For once, she had to employ logic and not let silly notions cloud her judgment. There had been no signs to guide her. And yet she needed none; her path was clear. It was the only path she could take. She would do better focusing on what she could gain from it, rather than on what she would lose.

She sat up and smoothed her hair. Leaving was the best course of action for everyone, including Orion and Lady Lindenshire.

If she stayed in London, people would assume she was Orion's mistress, no matter how vehemently they denied it. But if she left with the jewels, the *ton* would discover she was Gypsy, and they would assume the worst, as people always did. They would come to believe she had planned the entire deception, that she had taken advantage of the Lindenshires' good intentions and deliberately played the part of Lindenshire's dissatisfied mistress in order to steal the gifts of the hopeful protectors.

It wasn't stealing, though. It wasn't. The diamonds were hers to take. They had been given to her freely. She had paid dearly for them, for they had cost her her reputation, something she could not recover now, whether she returned the diamonds or not.

So the *ton* would believe the Lindenshires had been fooled, rather than believing they'd been flaunting custom in such a shocking way.

Ah, but what would the Lindenshires believe?

She would never know, because she would never see them again. And the imagined expression upon Orion's face would always haunt her dreams.

When she emerged from her chamber at last, she discovered six more packages the servants had left. As she opened them, joy swept through her like a spring breeze. It still wasn't a very large fortune, but it was more than she thought she would have, and if she lived very frugally, she could rear Anna properly in America and perhaps even provide her with a small dowry.

Her plan was set.

The weather had turned even colder, and she put on her warmest shawl before she went downstairs. There was much to do before she left England forever, and she had no time to waste, for she had only two full free days before Lady Lindenshire would arrive.

The time flowed past her with merciful swiftness. Two days left her little time to dwell on anything. She kept busy purchasing traveling clothes for herself and for Anna, arranging transport to Truro, and discreetly selling three of the brooches. As she made preparations, she watched for a sign to reassure herself she was doing the right thing, but no sign, no omen, no portent appeared. They had deserted her completely since she'd arrived in London, which she took to be a sign unto itself, a sign meaning London wasn't her destiny.

On her final night in London, she found herself completely alone. All but one manservant and the cook had gone to help at the countess's house for the day, and a wildly heavy snow had fallen, stranding them there and blanketing the city with a white hush. For once, London was silent, and, as she sat near the fire in Orion's library, she almost wished it were not. She would have welcomed some distraction from the task before her: to write a letter to Orion and his mama.

Putting it off for a moment more, she wandered aimlessly to the tall window and looked out at the dark sky. A break in the clouds revealed a bright ring around the full moon. There would be good light for late travel, should the need arise. She had hired a private coach, and she wished to be as far from London as possible by tomorrow night. She sighed and turned, dipped one of Orion's quills and sat at his large, well-equipped desk.

*My Dear Lady Lindenshire and—*

And who? "Lord Lindenshire" was too formal, "Orion" too informal. In the end, she crumpled the foolscap and began on a new sheet, having opted for the formal addresses on the outside and for "My Dear Friends," on the inside. They *were* dear to her, both of them.

After she employed her pen to explain how the events

of the last days in London had unfolded—how she had blundered her way into such a horrible bumble broth—she faltered. That had been the easy part. She tapped the quill and smoothed the feathery tip over her lips, deep in thought before writing more:

> *I am sorry for the trouble I have caused, and apologize sincerely. Please believe that I would never deliberately do anything harmful to either of you and that I am so very sorry at the turn of events my ignorance has produced. Though my actions were entirely innocent and born of a desire to be of service to you both, I am horribly aware that I may have brought you nothing but undesirable attention, if not outright humiliation, and I desperately desire to repair the damage I have done.*
>
> *Please know that you both hold very special places in my memory.*

She stilled. There was more to her feelings, but how to express it? Those at Stonechase Manor had always meant so much to her.

> *Always, no matter where the Gypsy caravan rolled, I knew you were still there, back at Stonechase.*

She paused. What she really wanted to say was that she'd known *Orion* was there. She wanted to say that she had *felt* him there, that she hadn't needed any signs to tell her he was still there. They'd been born on the same day, and she'd always felt an uncanny connection between them, like a string pulled taut. But she knew he would not welcome such an assertion, and she did not know what purpose it could possibly serve.

She sighed and got up to pace the room, words swirling with emotion, until she had put them together into some sort of coherent string of thoughts.

> *Though my world was fluid and unstable, I knew yours was solid and steady, from which I drew great comfort as the years passed. I hoped that someday I might see you again. And then the signs brought me to you. But now, for once, there are no signs, and I am—*

What? She was sorry to leave England forever without even saying good-bye? Sorry she was leaving with the jewels—and leaving the *ton* with the impression that the Lindenshires had been duped?

She covered her face with her hands.

Should she explain about Anna? Darling Anna, with her chubby hands and happy smile. Sweet baby Anna, who couldn't help it if her father was married but her mother was not . . . poor Anna! And poor Mama! She'd been so in love, and she was such a good soul that she hadn't been able to be unhappy, even when she found she was with child.

But would Lady Lindenshire and Orion understand that? And did Artemis have any right to divulge such a private matter to them? To take a chance on sullying her mother's memory?

No.

And yet she had to give *some* explanation for her behavior. She sat thinking again and then began once more:

> *I am convinced that my continued presence in London could only serve to damage how others view you both, and so it is with great regret that I leave London early on the morrow. The sooner I leave, the sooner the scandal will die. I will not be seeing you ever again, which grieves me more than you know. I know taking the jewels is not the proper thing to do, but I must because there is someone else depending upon me, someone dear to my mother whom I promised to care for in her absence, and now I have no other means.*
>
> *Thank you both for everything. I will never forget the*

*kindness and friendship you have shown me, and I will*
*be forever*

> *Yours devotedly,*
> *Artemis*

In truth, there was nothing more to say.

She sealed the envelope and left it on Orion's desk.

It was late. The sky had clouded over once again, and outside an owl gave two mournful hoots, while inside the sounds of the mantel clock dueled with the hissing of the fire for dominion over the silent house. Her baggage, what little she had of it, was waiting by the door for an early start. She would have no rest in the racing coach on the morrow, and she knew she should seek her bed, even though she suspected she'd have little sleep.

She turned to go upstairs but hesitated, trailing her fingers over the leather arms of Orion's chair. He would sit right there many times in the future. Would he ever think of her and wonder where she was? Her fingers skimmed over his desktop as her feet carried her to the table behind his desk. She touched his quill again, his blotter, his brandy carafe. She touched one or two books, his green velvet drapery, the window ledge.

And once more her eyes sought the sky. But for the snow clouds, the window would have offered a view of the constellation she knew so well. Orion, the great hunter, the only mortal man to have chased down Artemis. Even if Orion could forget her, she would never forget him, for the stars would always be there to remind her.

And then, for a brief moment, the cloud cover broke, and a star shone forth, the one at the Hunter's left shoulder.

Suddenly her skin prickled, and, sensing a movement behind her, she whirled about.

There stood Orion, silhouetted in the doorway, his face in shadow, as though she had conjured him with her thoughts. For a moment, she wondered if he were real, but then the sound of water dripping onto the floor assured her he was neither spirit nor fancy. He was sodden, and cold radiated from him like a hundred-year winter. He was wearing clothes suited for riding, not for travel in a carriage.

"My God, Orion! You were caught in this snow! Why did you not take shelter at an inn? Quickly, you must be warmed, or you shall catch your death." Robert, the only manservant left, was asleep, but she'd just have to wake him. She moved to reach for the bell cord.

"No," Orion said, stepping in front of her. "I feel no cold."

"But you must have dry clothes straightaway. Oh, dear . . . you were not expected, and your bedchamber will have no fire. I am afraid this is the only warm room in the house just now, save my own and Cook's. I will withdraw so that you can take off those—" She stopped, realizing the subject was indelicate to Orion's tonnish sensibilities. "The fire is banked. I will withdraw and send Robert to bring it to life and fetch you dry clothing." She made to leave, but he caught her wrist in a grip that was surprisingly hard.

"No. I wish you to stay." He dropped her wrist, kicked the door shut, and locked it. "This fire will do. And I have no need of clothes."

"But . . . well, we should not be alone. I am afraid there is no one here but Robert and Cook, and they are both asleep."

"Worried about propriety, my dear?" He scoffed, his voice and eyes were hard, and Artemis suddenly collected he was thunderously angry.

"Heavens, Orion. What is the matter?"

Pulling off his wet brown greatcoat, he let it drop to the floor and took one menacing step toward her.

Of course he was angry, she realized. There was only one reason for him to have ridden to London at night in weather like this: the gossip concerning her must have reached him. She squared her shoulders. If that were the case, it was best to take the bull by the horns. Once he understood what had happened, his anger would subside.

"You are angry with me," she began.

"Oh, no, my dear! How could I possibly be angry with so devoted a mistress?" As he spoke those sarcastic words, he unbuttoned his coat and untied his cravat. Then he swept them both off in one smooth motion.

The notion struck her that he might just take off every last stitch of his clothing. *Ridiculous,* she thought, *Orion would never do something like—*

He shrugged out of his ruined waistcoat and pulled his white linen shirt over his head, exposing a vast expanse of muscled chest.

Shocked into silence, she could only stare.

"What?" he asked sardonically. "Never thought to see your lover's naked body?"

"Orion!" Coming to her senses, she whirled about, turning her back, her cheeks flaming. "What are you saying?" She heard the shirt slide from his fingers and onto the floor. "You and I both know I am not your mistress . . . that we have never—stars and signs, Orion, we have never even kissed!"

"Ah, yes, but since everyone else in London believes we have, I believe it is high time we did. Don't you?"

Her pulse leapt in her throat. "You jest most cruelly, Orion."

"You think I jest?" he said, placing his strong hands on her shoulders and turning her about. His grip was not gentle. His brown eyes glinted coldly in the dim lamplight. He was bigger than she was, faster than she was—and angrier than she had ever seen him. She knew anyone with any sense ought to be afraid, but, to her own complete surprise, she wasn't.

"Nonsense. You do not even like me, Orion. You never have."

"Like? Perhaps not. But I do desire you."

"Oh?" she asked, sure he was jesting now, but the assertion made her feel breathless anyway.

"Yes, and you feel the same way about me."

She scoffed, though his words hadn't a shred of untruth in them. She *did* find him attractive. Any woman in her right mind would find him desirable. And seeing his bare shoulders, chest, and belly certainly hadn't done anything to diminish such feelings in Artemis.

Good Lord, she'd had no idea just how masculine his body really was under all that linen! Now she knew she'd never forget. The image of velvety-looking skin stretched smooth over powerful muscle and angular bone was seared into her memory like a brand. Drops of moisture glistened upon his taut skin, sparkling like tiny jewels, and his scent, a clean mixture of man and leather and soft cologne, curled its way into her consciousness like the warmth from a campfire, urging her to relax even as his words fought to raise alarm.

"Indeed!" she said, keeping her voice carefully even. "And how have you come to such a mad conclusion?"

He gave a mirthless laugh and said, "Can you not read the signs, Gypsy?" Grasping her hand, he pulled her over to a gilded mirror. Standing behind her, he flattened his cool, satiny palms against the sides of her head and forced her to look into the mirror with him.

He was standing too close. She could feel his warm breath against her bare shoulder and neck. His wide chest brushed her shoulder blades.

"See?" he said, his golden eyes meeting hers in the glass and flashing with intensity. "You are flushed. Your breathing is rapid, heavy. And—look!—your eyes keep flicking to my mouth. You want me to kiss you, Gypsy. Do you deny it?"

A fleet denial did spring to her lips, but it faded before she could utter it. It would have been a lie. How many times had she dreamed of kissing him? She dropped her gaze to her hands. "I do not deny it," she whispered.

Spinning her around, he roughly pulled her into his arms and took her mouth in a hard, demanding kiss. The scents of masculine cologne and exertion vied with the feel of his massive body pressed against hers, powerful and big.

She shouldn't have kissed him back. She should have pushed him away. But she didn't. Instead, she allowed all of the past sixteen years' uncertainty and isolation fuse with the fear, grief, excitement, frustration, sadness, and hope she'd felt since coming to London, and she kissed Orion with all the emotion she had kept tightly bound suddenly unleashed, and it was heavenly.

Caught somewhere between desire and anger, Orion finally came to his senses and broke the kiss. Lifting his head, he clasped her to him and looked into the mirror. She was still clinging to him, her back to the mirror, her black hair wound through his fingers. Her body was warm, pliant. Instinctively, he knew she was his for the taking. They were alone. He could lower her to the floor and—

Is that what he wanted?

He felt dazed, confused. He'd thought to punish her. He'd thought she'd resist his improper kiss. He wouldn't have been surprised if she'd struck him; he deserved it. He had expected a scathing protest, a heated scolding.

Her actual response stunned him.

He didn't know what to say. He'd been angry beyond measure. By the devil, he still was! He was ready for a fight, not for—

"Are you weeping?" He lifted his hand to her chin and tipped her face up to his. Though she met his gaze boldly, her tears continued to fall. "I detest tears. What is the matter? You wanted me to kiss you, and I did, by Jove!"

"You have kissed me in my dreams," she whispered,

"but not this way, not when you are angry. It is most cruel of you, Orion."

"Cruel?" Something inside Orion snapped, and his mind cleared. She was manipulating him. His heart turned to ice, and he thrust her from him. He moved to his desk, extracted his spectacles, and put them on. "Cruel," he murmured. "So *I* am cruel?" He laughed mirthlessly as he sat and steepled his fingers. "Shall I tell you what is cruel? It so happens I was given a lesson in cruelty today. Mama and I sat down to luncheon today with a Town pug who stopped by Stonechase on her way to Salisbury. And, of course, while she was there, she regaled us with the latest London *on-dits*. Mama and I were stunned to hear of a certain bird of paradise who had caused all tongues to wag by attending a cyprians' ball for the purpose of openly seeking a new protector. We were even more shocked to hear that this 'lady' was presiding over the town house of her current protector."

"Oh, no."

"Oh, yes. The pug enjoyed telling the tale. And all the while it was obvious she was building to a crescendo. We both knew there would be a startling crux to the story. Mama and I were on the edge of our seats. Can you imagine how I felt—how Mama felt?—when the pug gleefully confessed the name of the bold and vulgar woman who dared flaunt herself so?"

Artemis winced. "I can explain."

He sneered. "Do not bore me with your explanations. Logic has not abandoned me, I assure you, and I already know what you have to confess. You had the entire thing planned before you came to us in Stonechase. Bells and doves indeed! You actually expected me to believe such nonsense." He scoffed. "You counted on my mother's former friendship with yours, knowing she would find you a position in her household."

Artemis snatched the letter she'd written from the desktop and handed it to him.

"What is this?" he demanded.

"A letter to you and Lady Lindenshire. I wrote it earlier tonight."

He looked at her doubtfully.

"Please," she said. "Read it, Orion."

He tore the thing open and scanned it quickly, his brow furrowing deeper and deeper with each paragraph. Finishing, he tossed the letter onto the desk and shook his head. "This proves nothing. Likely you wrote it hoping to garner our sympathy and head off an investigation."

"What is there to investigate?" Artemis put her hands up in a gesture of supplication. "Surely you do not imagine I could have planned all this? How could I have known your mother's companion would run away or that there would be a fire at your mother's town house? That I would be forced to live here?"

"I suspect you have a compatriot who set the fire. Gypsies work in pairs and threes, it is said. And, please Artemis, 'forced'? You were not forced, you took advantage of whatever opportunities were presented you. Not that I blame you. You have lived as a Gypsy, and a Gypsy you shall always be, living by your wits, taking whatever fortune life deals you and finding some way of turning it to your advantage. No, I do not blame you, but neither can I admire you." He was surprised, for a moment, to see a look of hurt appear in her eyes, but in the next moment he realized she was an expert at such maneuvers. She was attempting to manipulate him again. It would not work. "You must have been astonished to find yourself showered with diamonds."

"You know about those?"

"How could I not? The pug's intelligence was startling in its completeness. My dear, every detail is wagging upon every tongue. Every London gossip is aware that my mistress has taken up residence—without my knowledge—in my own town house, and every London blood is aware you are seeking a new protector. I hear the bucks crowded the jewelers after you placed yourself on display at that ball the other night. They were all vying with each other to purchase the gaudiest, most tasteless trinkets and be the first to deliver them. I have to extend you credit. Your execution was brilliant. Not accepting any of them and putting them off with claims of a megrim gave more players time to get into the game. How many men have stepped forward. Six? Eight?''

"Thirteen," she murmured.

"Oho! An unlucky number," Orion said. "How unfortunate for you! I am rather surprised you planned to leave without waiting for number fourteen to press his suit."

Her eyes grew wide and flicked toward the door.

"Oh, yes—I took note of the baggage there in the hall. You must be feeling some urgency to leave. What else are you making off with besides the diamonds and the expensive clothes you did not pay for? My silver, perhaps? A cravat pin or two? Pray accept my apologies, my dear. I dislike jewelry, and I humbly regret that I have so little for you to steal." The look of shock on her face confirmed his suspicion. "You are nothing more than a common thief." Expecting her to show a guilty flush, he was surprised to see her bluster instead.

And then, suddenly, like a wonderfully defiant little beetle facing a hungry bird, she stood up to him.

"I had a very good reason for leaving! Were my own desires all that mattered, I would have chosen to remain as your mother's companion, to be near her—and you, though I do not now know why!—here in London, or at Stonechase, or wherever you happened to be. Wherever you were would have been good enough, but now—" She dashed a tear from her face and muttered, "Stars and signs, I do not know if I am more hurt or more angry." She shook her head and, drawing herself up to her full height, she leveled upon him a baleful expression. "I am not a thief, Lord Logic."

Quick as a flash, she stomped to the door, unlocked

it, and disappeared down the hall. He pursued and found her kneeling by her baggage near the front door, pulling garments from her huge, new-looking trunk and tossing them over her shoulder and into the air. Gowns, boots, shawls, and stockings fluttered and thudded into an untidy puddle about her.

"What are you doing?" he said.

"Showing you I am not a thief." She emptied the trunk and the two large bags next to it and then turned with a scowl on her face. "Look," she commanded, pointing into the trunk and the bags. "See for yourself."

He did look. The baggage was empty, save for a mound of winking diamonds at the bottom of one of the red-satin-lined bags. He picked it up. Brooches, necklaces, and bracelets. None of the jewelry was his, and not a piece of silver in sight.

"Go on, count them," she urged.

"What will counting them—"

"Oh, very well, I shall save you the trouble. There are ten. There were thirteen. One I sold for travel expenses, and two I sold to pay what I owed for these clothes." She gave her gown a vicious swipe. It was a deceptively simple yet elegant blue muslin creation cut in the latest style, and Orion knew the beastly expensive Madame Aneault would have charged dearly for it.

He scowled. "You are saying the mantua maker has been paid? That you yourself have paid her?"

"Yes."

"I do not believe you."

"Orion, I have never told you an untruth. Never. Although . . ."

She gave a guilty flinch, and a wave of revulsion assaulted Orion. He hated what he was doing, forcing her to lie to his face. He wasn't even certain why he was doing it.

"I have not told you everything," she finished and hung her head. "I have committed a lie of omission, for I have not told you the most important reason why I must leave London without delay."

"Oh?" He gave a deliberately sardonic lift of his eyebrows and braced himself for another spate of lies.

"I have a child to care for," she said. "A baby."

# CHAPTER SEVEN

Nothing she could have said could have surprised him more—or stopped him in his tracks faster. "A baby?"

She nodded.

Shock flooded his senses. Artemis, a mother? With a baby? A tiny baby? Where was it? Was it a boy or a girl? Why had she left the babe? Where had she left it and with whom?

*With her husband, perhaps?*

A sudden, irrational, yet undeniable jealousy stabbed him. And then, just as quickly, he regained his sense. Shoving such emotion aside, he tried to think. Why hadn't she mentioned her husband? Another jolt of shock coursed through him. Perhaps she did not have a husband. She might have been widowed—or never married at all.

"Where is the baby's father?" he asked.

"I am uncertain."

She avoided his gaze, and a wave of sympathy swept Orion's soul. She looked suddenly quite fragile. In Orion's imagination, the soft, fine muslin was replaced by her old coarse Gypsy clothing. He imagined her discomfort as the rough cloth chafed against her swollen belly. He wondered if they'd been camped when she'd given birth, or if she'd had to endure a jolting coach ride as her babe had come into the world.

His jealousy mixed with a cold, hard anger at the blackguard who'd bedded and then abandoned her.

Artemis sighed, breaking into his thoughts. "My mother did not tell me which of the brothers was Anna's father."

"Your mother?" He shook his head. "I do not understand."

"My mother gave birth eleven months ago, Orion. Anna's father was one of two brothers—Mama would not say which."

Orion heaved a sigh. So the baby did not belong to Artemis; it belonged to her mother! "The baby is only your half sibling," he said, relieved.

He watched as angry defiance claimed her. "She is my *sister*," she said. "*My* baby sister. And my charge. And I will not abandon her. She is mine to love, and it is my sacred duty—my sacred honor—to care for her. I promised Mama I would, and I will." She snatched the bag back from him and shook it. The jewels gave a crystalline jingle as they clinked together. "I will not give up this chance Fate has given Anna just because my taking the diamonds happens to offend your fashionable sensibilities, my lord. They were given to me freely, and I can do with them as I will." Her eyes blazed, her nostrils flared, and her lovely chest heaved with every indignant breath.

Orion gave a relieved sigh. "So you are not a thief."

"Of course not!"

"And you did not lie."

She only scowled.

Her story was true. Her explanation satisfied him, and her lovely indignance was real. Orion laughed with relief.

"I am happy you are amused, my lord."

Orion raked his hand through his damp hair and shook his head. "Ah . . . I have treated you abominably. Forgive me, Artemis. I was rippingly angry—"

"How dreadfully silly of me not to have noticed."

He smiled at her sarcasm. "—and I am sorry. Believe me, I am very glad to have been wrong about you."

"Dreadfully wrong."

"Yes, Gypsy. Dreadfully, idiotically, unforgivably wrong. I am ashamed I made such rash assumptions, and I apologize. Especially for my . . . my ungentlemanly behavior. I—" He looked down at his hands and then, with reluctance, back at Artemis once more. "May I speak freely?"

"You have so far," she said, her clear blue eyes full of suspicion.

Her wariness pained him. It was a direct result of his ineptitude. For once, he hadn't waited to gather all the evidence he needed to back his hastily drawn hypothesis. Ever since he had barged in and kissed her as though she were some sort of strumpet, she had given him nothing but the truth, and now she deserved nothing less from him.

"I was not lying when I said I am drawn to you. It seems we have both been dancing about such feelings, avoiding mention of them. And that is as it should be. We are complete opposites, you and I. We would not suit, Artemis."

He was relieved she did not attempt to deny an attraction—his own or hers.

Instead, she nodded. "It is true. We are like water and oil."

"Yes. Quite." He rubbed the back of his neck. "And yet, having kissed . . . well, things could now turn deucedly awkward between us, don't you think?"

"They could, yes."

"Dash it all, Artemis, I do not wish for that to happen. In spite of being water and oil, as my mother puts it, in spite of not bumping along in complete agreement from time to time, we have always been friends.''

"La, Orion, we can still be friends. It was just a simple kiss,'' she said with a dismissive wave of her hand, though, in reality, Artemis could think of nothing simple about it. Her own thoughts were in a whirl, at sixes and sevens, while she knew very well Orion's mind was ticking along with its usual well-ordered detachment. Of course it was. *He* had not spent several thousand nights in a wagon dreaming of *her*.

"When you arrived, you were freezing cold, bone-tired, and angrier than I have ever seen you,'' she said. "And on top of that, you had good reason to fancy I was a thief.''

"Not good enough.''

"Nevertheless, I am willing to forgive you. Let us pretend nothing happened. No one knows about that silly kiss but us. In fact, no one even knows you are here but me. It shall be our secret.'' She forced herself to smile. "Friends?''

"Friends,'' he agreed with a sigh. He sat heavily. "Come, Gypsy, tell me everything. Start from the beginning.''

"Not until you put on some clothes,'' she said.

"Afraid I will catch cold and die?''

"No.''

"Afraid you will be overcome with desire and die?''

"Hardly.'' She laughed. "I am more afraid I shall die of fumes. You stink.''

He tousled her hair. "Be serious, Gypsy. We have real problems on our hands.''

"I am serious. You stink.''

In spite of having changed into warm clothes, poor Orion still looked cold as he shivered before the reawak-ened library fire. Artemis was pleased to see he had put on his spectacles, for she took it as evidence he felt safe with her.

At close on two-o'-the-clock, the snow was still falling, but instead of the heavy swirls that had heralded his arrival, there was now but a slow, steady fall. The wind had died, the windowsills were filling with white, and the windowpanes above had begun to frost over.

While Orion had changed, she had built up the fire. Its popping and hissing light filled the room with a cozy glow. Artemis paused to watch him inhale the fragrant steam rising from his teacup. His spectacles fogged, and he closed his eyes.

"I confess," she said, continuing their discussion of the Viscount Whitemount, "he reminded me of a pretty snake—beautiful but unpredictable. I did not trust him at first, but then he was able to tell a tale or two from your time in school together. He presented himself as though you had a long-standing friendship."

Orion shook his head. "Not a friendship, but a rivalry. From the day we met, Whitemount has always been second to me, and it needles him. He would like nothing better than to disgrace me in the *ton's* eyes, and taking my own mistress from me certainly qualifies. I will likely never regain the position I have lost."

She shook her head. "I do not understand. Surely you do not imagine I accepted Whitemount's protection!"

"No." He sighed and sipped his tea. "No. Not at all. It is just that—well, it is dashed difficult to explain to one unfamiliar with the *ton*."

"Try," she urged. "I am not as lack-witted as you think."

He shook his head. "You know I have never thought you lack-witted." He sighed. "How to begin? You have noticed I have become a man of fashion."

"Of course." Artemis nodded, thinking to herself that he wasn't just a man of fashion; he was an unbelievably handsome and masculine man of fashion, and she found herself wondering what might have happened if he hadn't put his clothes back on . . . if he had gone on kissing her . . . if she had allowed—she jerked her mind back to what he had said. "Yes, um . . . yes, you are a man of fashion. A dandy."

"Yes," he answered.

"An exquisite?"

He nodded.

"A coxcomb?"

He frowned.

"A frippery-minded fop?"

His brows slammed together. "Now see here!"

She giggled. "I jest, Orion. Go on."

He threw her a black look spoiled by a pair of deep dimples, and then continued. "As I told you back at Stonechase, that day when we visited the ruins, I have not always been this way. I was as you remember me— with my nose forever in a book and my mind on my insects—until about two years ago."

"And then?"

He looked embarrassed. "And then I grew tired of being laughed at, of being thought of as some sort of scientific oddity."

"So you changed your outward appearance."

He nodded. "For two years, I dressed fashionably and attended a few events in Town here or there, but I did not truly bend my mind to the problem until three months ago."

"A lady," she said. "You fell in love with a lady, and you lost her. Your mama told me. Pray forgive her. She meant no harm, I am certain."

"I lay no blame at her feet. Rumors concerning me are difficult to avoid hearing. If she had not told you, I am certain someone else would have."

It seemed he might say no more, so Artemis prompted him. "And so . . ."

Still, he said nothing. The subject was obviously a sore spot with him.

She sighed. "And so you lost this lady to a gentleman

who enjoyed society's regard. A very manly gentleman. One you did not entirely approve of—one who did not care one whit about insects and who made your own interest in them seem rather . . . *un*manly. Correct?''

He looked startled. ''How did you know that? No''—he held up his hands—''I do not wish to hear it.''

She laughed. ''There were no cards or tea leaves involved, silly. Just a good guess. You are not the most inscrutable of mysteries, you know.''

''Meaning?''

''Meaning that I know you quite well, Orion. You may have put on fancy clothes and grown a little—''

''A little!''

She grinned. ''—but you are still the same Orion I knew as a girl. I knew you then, and I know you now.''

He shook his head and rolled his eyes. ''You guessed.''

''I did guess accurately, did I not?''

He gave a reluctant nod.

''Well then,'' she said, ''would you rather concede I know you, or would you, prefer that my tea leaves and crystal balls are to credit?''

He grinned. ''You know me. Too well,'' he added with a grin. ''And now that you have forced me to make that embarrassing admission, shall I go on with the story, or do you wish to guess the rest?''

''Let me see . . . after your heart was broken, you bent all of your considerable intellect toward becoming 'a man of fashion'?''

''Correct, more or less.'' He nodded.

''I see.''

''I think not, for there is much more to tell. Before you sidetracked me by dredging up my rather pathetic past—''

''Three months ago might as well be yesterday, Orion.''

''—I was attempting to explain why I cannot regain my position in Society.'' He tapped the rim of his teacup thoughtfully. ''Back to Whitemount. Because I am at the pinnacle of Society's regard, my mistress—you, as far as the *ton* knows, Gypsy—is, by association, at the pinnacle of every man's desire. Simply put, they all want to steal you from me.''

''Ah . . . so that explains why I am an object of such intense interest. I wondered. I received so many offers simply because they all thought I was yours.''

A curious warmth came into his eyes and he said, ''Not just that, Artemis. You are very . . . different. The Town pug who brought the news to Stonechase called you an 'elegant Gypsy.' Mutually exclusive terms, or so the *ton* would see them. The seeming inconsistency alone is enough to entice them. It makes you a mystery and lends you enough attraction all on its own. The fact that you are mine makes you irresistible to them, Artemis.''

''But what does all of that have to do with why you cannot regain your status?''

''I am not explaining it very well, am I?''

''No. Perhaps your head is frozen.''

He reached over and gave her shoulder an affectionate shove. ''Silly girl.''

''I think I know what you are so ineptly trying to say,'' she said with a grin. ''What you mean is that those at the pinnacle of society's regard have a very long way to fall.''

''Indeed. And with all of London believing my mistress has thrown me over so spectacularly—presiding over my own town house, ordering a new wardrobe seemingly at my expense, and attending a cyprians' ball on the arm of my fiercest social rival—well, I am afraid I have fallen very far indeed.''

''I am sorry, Orion. I wish there were something I could do to repair the damage.''

They lapsed into silence for a time, watching the flames dance in the fireplace and sipping their tea. Finally, Orion shifted. ''There is something you can do,'' he said. ''Agree to become my betrothed.''

She stopped breathing. She couldn't have heard him right. "Your what?"

"My betrothed."

*His betrothed.*

Her hand dropped and her cup clattered to a rest—on its saucer, by some miracle, since she wasn't watching. Instead, her eyes were fixed upon Orion, who was still staring into the fire, as though he had asked nothing more remarkable than, "Would you like some tea?"

She had been perfectly willing to try to forget his strong embrace, the feel of his smooth skin under her fingers, his tender mouth against hers, though she knew she would be a complete failure. She could never forget the way he had kissed her. Never. She'd known their one kiss would haunt her dreams forever.

But now he was asking to marry her. They would wed, and she would spend forever in his arms! A sudden gladness overtook her, a joy she had never experienced. Orion loved her! He wanted to marry her! Her soul went soaring through the heavens.

He looked up. "The only way out of this tangle," he said, "is to pretend we are engaged for a month or two."

"Pretend . . ." she murmured, plummeting miserably back to earth. "Oh. Oh, yes . . . yes, of course." She sat numb, unmoving. He did not truly wish to marry her. He only wanted to stage a sham engagement to save his position as the pinkest pink of the *ton*. If they pretended to be betrothed, the *ton* would have to believe there had been a misunderstanding.

He settled into the plump green sofa more comfortably. "Yes," he said as though reading her thoughts. "It is the only solution. We will say you were staying here without me to order new furnishings. We will say it was to be a surprise for me, and that you were here with the knowledge and complicity of my mother. Otherwise, we will tell the truth: that the ball was a terrible misunderstanding. When they learn you are the granddaughter of an earl and see us behave just as a respectable betrothed couple would, this will all be forgotten. And when it is safe to do so, we will cry off the engagement."

She said nothing. What was there to add? His idea was flawless. Logical. Reasonable.

And so horribly unemotional.

"I . . . I suppose you are right," she finally said, fiddling with her tea to cover her state of mind. She would not allow him to discover the depth of her own feelings. What would he say if he discovered she had been about to accept his "proposal" with such joy in her heart? What would he say if she told him she loved him? She knew very well what would happen. He would be embarrassed. He would pity her. And he would avoid her forever more.

She had to distance herself from him somehow, and she knew one sure way to do that: mention the signs. "I . . . I would be more confident if there were a sign to steer by," she said.

"Rubbish."

"It is most curious, Orion. There have been no signs since I came to London."

"Of course there were no signs, Gypsy, for there never truly are any such—what?" He put his cup down and waved his hand in front of her face, but she barely noticed. She was staring over his shoulder out the window and smiling.

"They came back."

Orion swiveled about and stared out the window. "Who came back?"

"The signs."

"What signs?"

"Two hoots," she said, rising and clasping her hands together.

"Two *what?*"

"And a star over his heart."

"Whose heart?" he said irritably.

"And a ring!" Her heart beat faster, and she whirled around to face Orion, who was staring at her as though she'd sprouted antennae and wings. "Oh, Orion . . . can you not see?"

"I *am* wearing my spectacles," he said dryly.

"You know that is not what I mean. Orion, the signs! The signs have returned! You brought them with you. And I know what they are telling us to do."

"Dare I ask?"

She gave him her best, brightest smile. How could she not smile? She was feeling suddenly light and happy. "We should indeed announce our engagement, but"— she gave him a beatific smile—"we should not cry off. Oh, Orion! The signs have spoken to me, and they have told me that, beyond all doubt, the right thing to do— the thing I am destined to do—is to marry you. We will wed. Indeed, it is our *destiny* to wed!" She gave a little twirl.

"Rubbish! You know I do not believe in all that super- stitious sign nonsense. You cannot expect me to go through with marrying you simply because some bird tweeted outside."

"It was an owl. The wisest of birds. You should have been here. All was silent and covered in white, and into the silence he hooted—twice! Two hoots—not one, not three—two. A pair. A couple. And then there was the star. The clouds broke for an instant, and I saw it clearly, the star over Orion's heart—his *heart!* And the moon, Orion! It had a beautiful silver ring around it. Oh, do you not see? It was a wedding ring. A beautiful silver wedding ring. The signs have spoken."

"Oh, no, Gypsy, not to me they haven't." He held up his palm. "I told you, we could never suit. You agreed with me, remember? Marry you?" He laughed. "Us, marry? The very idea!"

"But the signs—!"

"I do not give a fig what the blasted signs say! I will not marry you, Artemis. Never. *Never in a thousand years!*"

As though the matter was irrevocably settled, Orion stirred his tea and took a calm, measured sip. "Now then," he said, taking out his watch, "we shall have to bundle you off to Mama's place before dawn. With the help of her butler, we can have you settled agreeably and leave everyone thinking you left here before I arrived. We shall arrange for *The Morning Post* to carry the announcement of our betrothal tomorrow morning—it is too late for this morning. You cannot keep the jewels, of course. I shall have to quietly buy them back, and you will return them."

"What about Anna?"

"We will send for your sister straightaway, of course. We shall let it be known she is your sister—though the true story of her birth we will not share, of course."

"You are not"—she hesitated—"not disapproving of Anna?"

His face folded into an expression of tender sympathy that made her heart melt. "Anna is but a tiny child. It is not logical to find her anything but entirely innocent. And your mother . . ." He sighed. "How can anyone sit in judgment of someone they do not know? I know how both you and my mother feel about her, and so I cannot imagine that she was anything but good."

"You are most kind."

"I am only stating fact, and it is a fact that the heart can steer us into the darkest of places, but still we walk on, willingly and even joyfully, as your mother did. Her pure heart could not be tainted by her fell destination. It would be foolish to believe her goodness simply evaporated because she took an unfortunate turn. Which, as you have said, was not unfortunate at all in her eyes— for Anna's existence and the love she had for the baby's father brought her joy."

"Thank you, Orion. You are wise, and I am grateful. But I am also aware that the rest of the *ton* will not feel the same as you do. We shall have to make up a story, or there will be speculation focusing upon us as Anna's parents.''

"You are correct. We must protect Anna from those who would ridicule her." He stood and walked to the window. "You say your mama took great care to conceal the truth of Anna's parentage even from the Gypsies. Therefore, I think it is best that we let everyone in Town believe your mother was married to a Gypsy man. There will be no one to refute the claim, unless your old caravan makes its way through West Sussex."

"Even if they did, no Gypsy would knowingly reveal the deception of another. We sometimes fight bitterly among ourselves, but to the Outsiders, we present a united front. Conceal the rifts among us: it is the only way we have survived."

"Would their allegiance extend to you?"

"Yes. Though I was never fully accepted, I was a member of the caravan, and Gypsies take hospitality seriously. Their code of honor extends to their guests—which is how I was viewed."

He nodded thoughtfully. "Sometimes, hearing you speak of them, I wonder if the rest of us could not learn from the Gypsies. Their sense of loyalty is humbling." His solemn expression reflected his sincerity.

It was on the tip of Artemis's tongue to mention that there were other things the *ton* could learn from the Gypsies—such as a belief in the signs—but just then the clock chimed a quarter past the hour of two.

Orion blinked. "Now then," he said, "back to the business at hand. We will settle very publicly into the roles expected of a betrothed couple. You will, in fact, redecorate my town house—sparing no expense, for the more is spent, the easier the deception will be swallowed. You will triple your order with Madame Aneault, and we will attend a few selected functions together. Eventually, when the mistress scandal has died, we will decide very publicly—and very amicably—to cry off. Since you are, in essence, giving up a fortune in jewels in order to

restore my own reputation, I will compensate you with
. . . say . . . two thousand pounds? My mama will retain
you as companion even so, and everything will be as it
should.''

''Very well. It all sounds quite reasonable,'' she said.
''Henceforth, we are betrothed then?''

He nodded. ''We are.''

Artemis smiled. She was engaged to Orion Chase!
And if he wanted to believe they would not be married,
that signified little, for she knew better. One could not
argue with the signs.

Artemis and Orion would be wed, and that was that.

# CHAPTER EIGHT

Orion thought everything was proceeding swimmingly—at first. With Peabody's help, Artemis was safely transferred to his mother's residence and installed in her bedchamber there even before the kitchen staff was awake. The butler's complicity would stave off any scandal concerning Orion and Artemis having been virtually alone in his town house at night. Orion explained things to Peabody, and that trustworthy man would ensure everyone believed Artemis's installation at the countess's house had occurred before Orion arrived in London.

Orion was able to buy back the brooches Artemis had sold very early that morning, and all of the jewelry was returned to her hopeful protectors before most of the *ton* were awake. With each package went a lengthy letter signed by Artemis and explaining that her presence at the cyprians' ball was due to a misunderstanding.

His mother arrived late that afternoon, and the *ton* was thrown into doubt. Was the Countess of Lindenshire unaware she was playing hostess to her son's wayward mistress, or had there been some mistake, as the letters said? Both Lindenshire households turned away a steady stream of disappointed callers that day.

The very air seemed charged with curiosity by the time *The Morning Post* brought the betrothal announcement to breakfast tables across London the next morning.

As he rode to his mama's town house early that afternoon, Orion was stopped several times by the barest of acquaintances, all transparently eager to wish him happy. None made any secret of knowing the exact content of the letters, and all were eager to ferret out some minute detail that would reveal a delicious chink in the armor of the story. They all came away disappointed, however, for Orion and Artemis had been quite careful, and no such flaw existed. Everything would come out right so long as they all—Orion, Artemis, his mother, and Peabody—stuck to their appointed roles.

He stopped by Brooks's Club on the way. There would still be a few stalwart stragglers from the night before at this time of day, and he knew his behavior there would be reported and passed from gentleman to gentleman throughout the day.

Sitting at a card table, he was immediately joined by three other Town bucks—holdovers from last night, by the look of them. They wouldn't have seen the morning newspapers yet. Mr. Jeremy Scott grinned lopsidedly and sat at his right. "So, Lindenshire, I hear you've managed to catch yourself quite a bird."

"From the highest treetop, too," said Samuel "Pink" Peplin, sitting across from Orion. "Too high for me to reach. Turned me down yesterday morning." He pulled from his pocket a small envelope and tossed it onto the table. It was addressed to "Mr. S. Peplin" in Artemis's tidy hand, of course. "'M' valet tracked me down with it. Think I'll dismiss the man," Pink said.

The third gentleman, Sir Edward Benton, laughed. "No shame in that, Pink. Talk is the bird's too flighty even for Lindenshire to hold on to. Wonder where she'll land.''

"At least you two danced with her," said Mr. Scott. "I couldn't even get near her at that ball, not with the rest of you dastards crowding round her like lads drooling over a cherry tart."

"A tart right enough, but I'll wager it ain't cherry," Sir Edward said.

"Oho! Not with the way she dances," Pink Peplin said. "Hips bobbing like they knew what they were doing. Thought she was going to take me right there on the—"

"Enough!" Orion stood up.

"Oh, come now, Lindenshire," Sir Edward said amicably. "Only a spot of fun."

"Yes," Pink said. "She's only a lightskirt. No need for heroics."

Orion leaned over the table. "One more word about that 'lightskirt,' and I will offer to show you the business end of a pistol at Bethnal Green—or a sword, if you would prefer. I would choose the sword, were I you, for I cannot merely scar you for life with a pistol. I would have to kill you instead."

During the shocked silence that followed, Orion realized he meant every word. Artemis may have been a fake fiancée, but she was a true friend, and he would not sit back and let her be maligned no matter what these Town bloods thought his connection to her was.

The two men sitting at his side had the sense to look appropriately nervous. They had good reason. It was the fashion for a man to be a crack shot, a brute in the ring, or a competent fencer, if he could manage it. Orion had been willing to work hard at becoming fashionable, and he'd discovered some natural talent in the physical arts he hadn't known was there. Though he was not the best boxer at Gentleman Jackson's, he was a good enough shot to be considered formidable on the green at dawn, and he was deadly accurate with a rapier. All in all, a man not to be crossed.

And yet, in spite of Orion's well-known talents, Pink Peplin, whether too sleepy, too foxed, too stupid, or too full of himself, laughed too carelessly—though his cravat pin was winking at his throat in rapid time to his leaping heartbeat. "You would draw blood over a lightskirt, Lindenshire?"

"No, but I would draw blood over a lady."

"A *lady?*" Pink sneered.

Orion thundered. "Miss Artemis Rose is a lady. And my fiancée, as you would know if you had read this morning's *Post*."

Pink's jaw dropped open. "F-fiancée!" he stammered. "I say! Had no idea, Lindenshire. Must have been some mistake. Terribly sorry. Terribly sorry!"

The three men looked expectantly up at Orion, who held Pink's gaze just long enough to put the fear of doubt into his mind before sitting easily down once more. "No harm done," he said. He motioned to a serving-man. "Brandy," he ordered and then picked up the deck of cards. "A game, gentlemen?"

During the game that followed, he laughed off the whole incident with what he was certain was a convincing aplomb, a performance that would have rivaled any of Edmund Kean's.

Orion soon discovered his mama and Artemis weren't having any problems at all playing their own parts, either. In fact, they were throwing themselves into their roles with disconcerting glee.

As he walked into his mama's sunny morning room an hour later, he spotted the two of them huddled together on the yellow damask sofa and poring over a stack of ladies' magazines. Artemis was dressed becomingly in a gown with a white bodice and pink skirt, a wide black sash at the high waist. It was an unusual style, but Orion thought it fetching and smart. Obviously, Madame Aneault found Artemis's small, curvy frame and cascade of dark curls an inspiring vector for her creativity.

Artemis patted the magazine on her lap, its pages butterflied open to the fashion plates. "Very well. What color shall I wear to the ball, then?" she asked his mother.

"Ah, yes, the betrothal ball . . . let me see . . ." the countess mused.

Inwardly, Orion groaned. The obligatory betrothal ball. Of course. The very idea filled him with dread. He knew that, in order to overcome the inertia of the *ton's* initial disbelief, it would not be enough simply to act as the average bored bridegroom. No, he would have to appear as a besotted bridegroom in public. But a blasted betrothal ball just seemed too blasted public! There wasn't any way to avoid the thing, though. Not having one would arouse suspicion—the last thing he needed.

"Red," his mama finally decreed. "You simply must be dressed in red. It is the color of love."

Orion frowned and cleared his throat.

"My darling boy!" his mama exclaimed, rising and picking up her sea-green skirts to rush over to him. "You have made me so very happy." She beamed at him and then at Artemis, who smiled like a cat locked in a creamery. Warning bells sounded in his head. Something wasn't right. "I have ordered tea," his mother said. "Come, come. Sit with us. We were just discussing the arrangements."

It was, of course, the first time he had seen his mother since their arrival in London. He'd been busy with finding, buying back, and returning the brooches, and then with staying out of sight until the betrothal announcement. Thus, Artemis had been the one to explain to her the circumstances leading up to their false betrothal—but, judging from his mother's expression of delight, the miserable chit hadn't explained it at all as Orion might have.

"Perhaps Artemis has not told you everything," he said, deliberately bland.

"Oh, yes, she has! Every detail. The owl, the star, the ring. A silver ring! Oh, dearest, do bring out the ring." Her eyes roved over his pockets, clearly looking for the telltale outline of a ring box. "You did purchase a ring this morning, did you not? That is why you are so late in coming today?"

"I have had other things to do this morning, Mama." Like sleeping late and dressing with more care than ever, since he'd known he would be scrutinized today at his club and on the street more heavily than he usually was.

"Oh, Orion! No ring? Well . . . I suppose that cannot be helped now, but you must rectify that mull before your betrothal ball, you know, and the gold of the ring simply must be white. A wedding ring must not be silver, of course, but Artemis saw a silver ring around the moon, not a golden one, and you do not wish to go against the signs, do you?"

Orion blinked. "The signs?"

His mother looked at Artemis. "He still does not believe."

Artemis shook her head. "I am afraid not."

His mother threw him a look of supplication. "It is her betrothal ring, Orion. She will have to live life with that ring on her hand, and it should be what she wants. Even you will have to agree with the logic of that."

*Hell and blast!* The two of them believed the wedding was going to happen! Orion was just about to open his mouth to deliver a blistering response when Peabody came in bearing tea. "Ah, Master Orion! I understand we will soon be celebrating your wedding. It is my pleasure to wish you both happy."

"Thank you, Mr. Peabody," Artemis said.

"Peabody," Orion said, "you know very well Artemis and I"— he lowered his voice—"are not going through with it. I explained things to you myself the night before last."

Peabody shrugged at the countess and winked at

Artemis before turning a more sober expression upon Orion. "Yes sir. You did, sir."

"Very good," Orion said. Peabody was a sensible, steady man. Orion trusted him completely. In spite of his conciliation toward the ladies, he would not swallow all of that sign nonsense as the countess had.

"Did you bring the extra teacup?" Artemis asked the butler.

"I did, miss." He produced the yellow flowered cup and set it down on the tea tray in front of her.

Orion gave a grateful smile, pleased Artemis had thought of him. He welcomed the tea, parched as he was. The journey from his club had taken him close to an hour—much longer than usual because he'd been flagged down so many times to be wished happy and to be interrogated.

Artemis patted the spot next to her on the yellow sofa and reached for the teapot.

Orion hesitated, wondering if sitting so close to a lady who thought she was going to marry him was entirely wise, but a second later he realized he needn't have pondered the matter at all.

"By your leave, ma'am?" the butler asked the countess.

"Oh, certainly, Peabody, sit down. She says you must drink it yourself."

Without so much as a glance at Orion, the butler took the place next to Artemis, who handed him the cup of tea.

Orion gaped, unnoticed, as Peabody gulped his tea eagerly and handed the empty cup back to Artemis. Frowning, he watched as she stared into the bottom of the cup, while the butler and the countess leaned in close, attempting to get a better look.

"What is going on here?" Orion cried, though he knew very well what he was witnessing.

"Shhh," his mother hissed. "Peabody's youngest

daughter is with child, and he wishes to know if the babe is a boy or a girl."

"Four children of my own and nine grandchildren so far and not one boy in the lot. Can you imagine, sir? I am going mad wondering about this latest."

The countess patted the old widower's hand. "Artemis gets very good results with the leaves."

"My fiancée is reading *tea leaves*?" Orion thundered, though he was unsure which shard of the whole broken picture disturbed him more: Artemis reading tea leaves, the butler's uncharacteristic and highly improper familiarity, or the fact that offering *him* tea hadn't once entered anyone's mind.

His mother gave him a baleful look. "What did you fancy she was doing, Orion, reading palms?"

"A boy!" Artemis cried. "The babe is a boy!"

"Thank goodness!" Peabody grinned.

"Oh, how splendid!" the countess said.

"Congratulations, Mr. Peabody!" Artemis set down the cup with a satisfied flourish.

"When is the child due to make his arrival?" the countess asked. "We will be sure the wedding date does not interfere with your ability to travel to greet the lad."

"Thank you, ma'am. Most kind of you."

"You have all gone mad," Orion said. "Peabody, Mother, once and for all, I do not believe in such nonsense. And our betrothal is false. I am not marrying Artemis!"

The three of them traded knowing looks, and then the countess spoke. "Yes, dear." She cleared her throat. "Now . . . what do you think about holding your *faux* betrothal ball at the Argyll Rooms? This house is much too small, and your house will be in the thick of being redone."

Orion silently counted to ten and gave up on the idea of convincing his mother that he would not wed Artemis. There was no use wasting his effort. No matter what he said, the stubborn woman wouldn't believe him.

"Orion?" his mother prompted him. "The Argyll Rooms?"

He sighed. If there had to be a betrothal ball, the thing for him to do was to take control of the entire affair right from the beginning. Otherwise, his mother would turn it into a champagne-spewing, cherub-sporting, red-rose-covered fête that would be talked of in wondering tones for the next decade.

"The Argyll Rooms," he mused. They could hold an enormous number of people, and he was certain his mother would fill them to the brim. He could just see Artemis reading tea leaves at the Argyll Rooms. No, the smaller the guest list, the better. Fewer witnesses. "The Argyll Rooms are where the largest of the cyprians' balls are held," he said. "I think that, under the circumstances, we may wish to avoid such an association in our guests' minds."

"Oh! Yes! Why did I not think of that?"

"Our country house is a better choice. Less opportunity for our guests to make *unpleasant* associations." And more privacy for Orion.

"Well," his mother said uncertainly, "Stonechase Manor cannot accommodate quite as many guests, but it will be close enough to Christmas to deck the place with green. How lovely! We shall invite the guests to stay, of course. A house party!"

Good heavens, a house party? Orion turned away to hide the roll of his eyes. He'd just maneuvered himself from a six-hour ball into a six-day house party. "Perfect," he muttered. "Just perfect."

"Yes," the countess cried, "it will be the perfect setting for your betrothal ball! Your *faux* betrothal ball, rather," she said with poorly concealed glee in her tone.

He knew very well his mother still imagined he and Artemis would wed. But he also knew most of the *ton* had already made plans for Christmas, and even if everyone accepted the invitation on such short notice—impossible, Orion thought—there would be only fifty or so, for that was all Stonechase would hold.

What he hadn't counted on was how devilishly persuasive his mother was—or how devilishly eager the *ton* was to greet his fiancée.

# CHAPTER NINE

A week before the betrothal ball, Stonechase Manor was stuffed full to the eaves. Every available bed was taken. Guests had been arriving for several days from far and wide. Orion didn't know of a single person who had refused the Countess of Lindenshire's invitation.

He should have felt at ease. Over the course of the past fortnight, much of the *ton's* initial skepticism had evaporated in the face of Artemis and his mother's sincerity. He did not feel at ease, however. In fact, he was deucedly out of sorts, for he knew why Artemis was so convincing. She wasn't playing a part at all. In spite of his open desire to remain single, she openly believed it was their true destiny to wed. She was stubbornly and happily making plans to marry him for real. And his mother was helping!

His town house, by all accounts, had been gutted and was even now swarming with workmen. The ladies had been cloistered with Madame Aneault at the mantua maker's salon the entire week before they returned to Stonechase Manor. They'd ordered a complete trousseau for Artemis, and expensive-looking boxes of gowns and fripperies had been arriving every morning for a week. Artemis had decided upon a menu for their wedding breakfast, an itinerary for their wedding trip, and the color of the roses she wanted filling the church.

And the hell of it was Orion could not stop her, did not want to stop her, because, were they truly engaged, those were the things she would logically be doing.

He couldn't wait for the ball to be over. Even though the *ton* seemed convinced, he knew some still harbored suspicion. Since the first volley of them had arrived at Stonechase that morning, nowhere on the grounds was he free of their scrutiny, their questions. They had descended like locusts and now roved over the estate like ants, poking into every cranny.

Needing some time to himself, he set out for the ruins, which were quite a distance away: over a gray stone footbridge, alongside the brook, through a thick copse of lindens, and finally up and then back down a long, sloping hill. It felt good to be outside. He didn't want to be cooped up in his bedchamber, and every other part of the house was crawling with guests. He needed the air and the exercise and the solitude, and the ruins were just the place to spend a pleasant hour alone with his thoughts.

But just as he gained the hill's apex, he saw far below a small party of guest-ants who had invaded the ruins. No good. Well then, he'd seek refuge at his "experiment place," as he'd called it when he was a boy. No footpath led there. Surely he would find solitude. Back down the hill, through the copse, a turn north, over the meadow, and down the embankment Orion hurried and then sighed with relief.

His experiment place was deserted.

He half slid, half walked down the embankment and sat on the protruding roots of the giant linden next to the brook. It was cold down there in the damp air of that sheltered spot, but he didn't care. But for the gurgling of the brook it was silent, blessedly silent and—

"Why, Lindenshire!" a nasally voice accosted him. "I thought that was you I saw hotfooting it over the grass!"

Orion turned. Up on top of the embankment, silhouetted against the bright midday sky, stood a portly baroness. "Lady Prichard," Orion greeted her with a polite bow, though he would rather have tossed her into the quick-flowing water.

"Has Miss Rose's sister arrived yet?" the lady said, referring to Anna.

"No, ma'am. We have not had the pleasure of welcoming her thus far."

"Oh." Her face contracted as though she were sucking a lemon. Seconds ticked by, and Orion thought she might leave, but then she spoke again. "Lovely weather we have, is it not?"

"Eh? Oh, yes . . . yes, lovely."

"Sky as clear as a bell."

"Mmm." Orion made a noncommittal noise, privately thinking it was rather hazy that day.

"So blue," Lady Prichard said.

"Indeed."

"Like Miss Rose's eyes."

He nodded. "Yes."

"And her sister's?"

"Ma'am?"

"Her sister's eyes . . . are they as blue as Miss Rose's are?" She gestured at the sky, as though the child could be found nestled among the puffy white clouds.

Orion didn't know what color Anna's eyes were. He hadn't thought to ask. "I do not know what shade you might say her eyes were," he averred.

"Mmm," the baroness mused. "A babe's eye color sometimes changes anyway. How about the hair?"

Orion didn't know what color Anna's hair was, either, and this time the baroness's question could not be so easily escaped. Unlike eye color, an infant's hair color was not wont to change.

"Well?" Lady Prichard prompted "You do know the child's hair color, do you not?"

They all thought he'd seen Anna before. He'd let them think he'd been reacquainted with Artemis for much longer than he had; otherwise, they'd never have believed the betrothal.

"Well, Lindenshire?"

He had to answer the question. And yet he could not answer the question, for what if he gave the wrong answer? For the space of three seconds, Orion bent his considerable intellect toward getting out of the pickle he was in. His eyes fixed upon a rock at the baroness's feet—a very familiar rock—and, suddenly, he knew just what to do.

"Hold . . . *very* . . . still," he said, keeping his eyes fixed on the rock.

Her eyes widened, and she looked wildly about her in fear.

*"Still!"* he ordered.

She froze in place.

Orion put his finger to his lips and whispered. "Do not move. I will remove it."

*"It?"* the baroness hissed.

"Shhhh!" Orion crouched and crept toward her, his eyes still fixed on the rock just next to her left foot.

Imagining God only knew what, the portly woman closed her eyes tightly shut.

*Perfect.* Orion knelt, tilted the familiar rock up, plucked out one of the insects he knew he'd find there, and deposited the thing atop the lady's reticule. "Drop your bag, Lady Prichard. Quickly!"

The lady opened her eyes and, looking down with a squeal, dropped the reticule and danced away.

"You had better leave the area, Lady Prichard, for there are probably more of them. I shall bring your reticule along later after the creature is gone. After *the swarm* is gone."

"Swarm!" The lady scooted back up the path and

out of sight, squeaking with alarm. Orion chuckled, but then he scooped up the reticule and strode back to Stonechase. Leaving the reticule in the care of Mr. Peabody, he beat a hasty path to his bedchamber, his last bastion of peace.

Thus it was that as Artemis's very presence turned his world upside down, he managed to hold on to his temper—until he found her and an army of drapers in his nice, simple, masculine bedchamber, decking the place in yellow flowered everything and sickeningly fancy feminine furbelows.

"Out!" He pointed to the door.

"Stay," she instructed the workmen, who glanced nervously and uncertainly from one to the other of them. "Orion? Dearest?"

"Out. Now," he said with a menacing quiet. Everyone scurried out the door. Including Artemis. *Smart girl,* he thought. But he wasn't about to let her get away.

He followed her down the corridor, and just as she was rounding a corner, he covered her mouth to prevent her from crying out and hauled her small pink-gowned frame back into his chamber. After releasing her, he closed the door and turned the key, which he tossed carelessly onto the bed.

"Orion! Someone might discover us! It would ruin the wedding!"

"Then you had better not raise your voice," he shot back.

"What has you so irritated?"

"You, Gypsy. You and your belief in destiny, our destiny. It is like a burr under the saddle or an annoying fly endlessly buzzing in one's ear, and I have had just about enough." He gestured about the room. "You have gone too far. This is my bedchamber, not yours." He grasped the newly hung drapery, jerked it down, and then ripped it in half, right before her eyes. "Mine, not yours. And it never will be yours. Understand?"

She cocked her head to one side and crossed her

arms stubbornly. "Do you dislike yellow, then? I can have it done in blue, if you wish. Or green. Green is a lovely color, very restful."

"You are being deliberately obtuse."

"Then we are evenly matched, for you are deliberately disregarding the signs."

"Yes!" Orion cried, forgetting for a second that he was supposed to be quiet. He lowered his voice. "You are right. I am. How can you be surprised at that? Let me clarify for you how I feel about your deuced, devilish signs! They are rubbish. They are nonsense. They are not rational, not logical, not reasonable. They have no bearing upon reality. They do not shape my destiny, because there is no such thing as destiny. No destiny, no fate, and no damnable way I will allow you to force me into marrying you just because some bird tweeted and the weather changed. A wedding ring around the moon. Bah! I would sooner marry a dung beetle. At least *they* do not pretend what they are rolling around in is truth!"

He expected her to scowl. He expected her to fume and pace and steam. But she didn't. Instead, she looked down at the ring he had given her—a yellow gold band with a large ruby—and turned it round and round on her finger.

"You are wrong," she whispered. "Peabody's daughter gave birth to a boy."

"One chance in two."

"It is not the only prediction I have made since we returned to Stonechase."

"Oh?" Orion scoffed. "Did you predict the sun would rise and set? That birds would fly, that people would blink?" He clapped his hands together and cried, "How famous!"

"I have made several predictions that did come true."

"Have you made any predictions that did not come true?"

"There *are* a few that have not happened—"

"Aha!"

"—yet." She stamped her foot. "Just because they have not happened yet does not mean they will not happen at all."

"If you make enough predictions, some of them will come true, Gypsy." Orion laughed derisively.

"You do not want to believe, so no matter what evidence I present you with, you never will."

"Never in a thousand years," Orion agreed.

Artemis snatched up the key and stuck her nose in the air. "I am going to the stable." She whirled away from him and, unlocking the door, marched out of the room, her chin high. "You stubborn little boy!"

"Silly girl."

The door shut with a *bang* behind her. Orion was peeved with her. He should have been scowling. But he was standing there grinning like an idiot instead. He had actually enjoyed provoking her. It had always been so.

He turned and, walking straight over to the wall, lifted one of the ornate moldings and depressed the latch hidden there. The wall swung inward, and he ducked into the opening. Behind the wall was a small space, his secret laboratory. It wasn't much of a laboratory, really little more than a landing within a narrow stair passage that led up to the attics and down to an escape tunnel below the cellars.

Parts of Stonechase Manor were extremely old. The house had been begun during a time when escape tunnels came in handy all too often. A later ancestor had constructed the passage up through the center of the house and connected the passage to the tunnel.

But the secret of the tunnel had been lost for unknown years until Orion had stumbled onto it once more. He had discovered the passage as a boy, and he'd kept it secret. It had been his refuge then.

"And it still is," he murmured, pulling off his itchy cravat and gloves. He had disabled every opening into the passage but the one leading into his bedchamber, and there wasn't a soul who knew of the passage. He'd never told anyone—except for Artemis, and he wondered if she'd forgotten, for she'd not mentioned it since she arrived. He could and did carry on with his research there, knowing there was no risk of discovery. He shrugged out of his coat and unbuttoned his waistcoat. The passage wound around one of the great Stonechase chimneys and was usually fairly constant in temperature at this level. Lower down, it was frigid no matter the season, while further up it was hellish. Here, though, it was warm in the winter and comparatively cool in the summer.

Perfect for his experiments.

He lit a pair of lamps and shut the outer door with a click, uncovered his microscope, and then drew forth two crates filled with glass boxes. He had work to do.

He had been in the middle of an important segment in the arc of his research when Artemis had shown up at Stonechase Manor. *Bells and doves indeed!* He lit a bright-burning candle and placed one of the glass boxes on the microscope's stage. He'd been glad to see her but dismayed to see his own mother so easily fooled by all that sign rubbish.

Peering into the microscope, he began counting and sorting the beetles, live on one side, dead on the other. *One . . . two . . . three . . .* they were such tiny things, looked so insignificant, so harmless. *Four . . . five . . . six . . .* and yet they could decimate an entire season's crop of corn in less than a week. *Seven . . . eight . . . nine . . .*

*Rather like Artemis,* he thought. She didn't look very persuasive, and yet she had pulled even his mother's dour-faced butler into her superstitious nonsense. *Ten . . . eleven . . . twelve . . . thirteen.*

He frowned at the unlucky number—and then frowned at himself. *Unlucky?* Had it really occurred to him that a simple integer was an unlucky omen? *Bloody deuced hell and back!* Just having her around was damaging. What was next? Would he be avoiding black cats and handing his palm over to be read?

One thing was certain: he wasn't going to be of any use up here, not with her on his mind. His research required concentration. Without it, he might miss some vital detail. He was looking for a way to eradicate the little corn beetle. It was important research, and he could not afford to have his attention divided.

How was he to regain his concentration, to exorcise that blasted Gypsy from his mind? Exorcise . . . exercise! That was it. Over the last two years, he'd become used to spending many hours at fencing and boxing and riding. He hadn't had much exercise since Artemis had come to Stonechase Manor, and he chafed at his current level of inactivity. Perhaps that was why he was finding it difficult to concentrate. Yes. It wasn't Artemis at all, but a lack of exercise. Fencing and boxing were out, but perhaps a good, hard ride would render him more cerebral.

On impulse, he grabbed the candle and crept down the stairs. His valet was elsewhere, and he didn't feel like spending a half hour retying his cravat, anyway. He'd just tie it loosely before he stepped outside, and—

"Miss Artemis said the signs have spoken to her." The muffled, tinny voice emanated from a small tube that poked down from the ceiling. The passage had several of the listening devices, and though he'd always known the passage could be used for eavesdropping or spying, Orion had rarely done so, even as a child. He'd always been more interested in the activity of insects than in the activity of people, and his only interest in the passage had been as a laboratory. He did not wish to eavesdrop; it was bad manners and entirely unethical, but hearing Artemis's name proved too formidable a lure. He bent close to the tube, listening.

"Accept Matthew. You dare not go against her signs, Maire," said a second, higher-pitched voice. *Alice.* She and Maire were the two downstairs parlor maids.

"Accept Matthew? Alice, dearie, Matthew hasn't two pennies to rub together."

"But you love him."

"Aye," Maire said with a sigh. "That I do. But what would we live on? It's Charles who has the fortune. Two hundred guineas!"

"Ah, but he might not ask you. Miss Artemis clearly said she saw four black swans and one white one in the brook, all chasing after a green fish. Surely that has to be Charles Green. And look in the mirror, Maire! You and your sisters are all black-headed, but your sister Catherine, she's as fair as the day, and 'twas the white swan that nabbed that fish."

"Yes. Well . . ."

"Matthew has asked you. It's Matthew you love. If you ask me—or Artemis—you'd be a fool to make Matthew wait for your answer until after you're sure Charles won't ask you. Matthew's a clever one; he'd be sure to guess what you're about, and he might get angry-like. You might lose him."

"I wish I could be sure Matthew will wait," Maire said.

"Why don't you ask Artemis?" Alice suggested. "I'll wager she could tell you."

"You think she'd see another sign?"

"Might," Alice said, "but mind she's good with tea leaves, too."

"Oh, and I saw her reading palms in the stables just this morning," Maire said, excitement building in her voice.

*Lovely,* Orion thought, *just lovely.* Now Artemis had the grooms and stable boys believing in all that nonsense. At least she had the sense to keep it away from the other guests.

Alice lowered her voice so Orion could hardly hear her. "Just be sure the master's not about when you ask Miss Artemis for help. She's been hiding it from him."

Maire giggled. "I know. She had one of the stable boys posted on watch for him while she read Lady Devonshire's palm this morning. Lord Lindenshire would be plum angry about that if he knew, and no mistake."

*No mistake.*

Orion didn't wait to hear more. He did not need to. He was already "plum angry" enough. He headed for the cellar exit, as he had at the outset. Only this time it had nothing to do with a desire to avoid having to fuss with his valet.

It was simply the fastest way to get his fingers round Artemis's delicate little neck.

# CHAPTER TEN

Artemis was tired. Reading palms was difficult work. It required such concentration, and, truth to tell, she had never felt terribly confident at it. She shifted on the upturned barrel she was sitting upon and rubbed the small of her back a little before returning to peer minutely at the outstretched palm of the gentleman sitting across from her.

She was a little better with tea leaves—or even with coffee grounds, in a pinch—and she was very good with spotting and interpreting the signs, but ever since Lady Devonshire had asked Artemis to read her palm that morning, a steady stream of guests had made their way to the stables. After the third or fourth reading, she began to suspect they were as fascinated with the idea that she might be hiding the readings from Orion as they were with the readings themselves.

She almost wished she had not posted a guard to watch for her betrothed.

Almost.

Oh, but these people were so in need of her help! The tonnish house guests were much less aware about their own lives than the servants were about theirs. They paid little attention to the true needs of others, and even less to the true needs of their own bodies.

Artemis advised one to move his favorite chair into his grandchildren's nursery and another to consume less cream and more fish. But, unlike the servants, the guests did not seem to want her help with love affairs.

She'd found herself frowning more than once about that. The *ton*, it seemed, did not consider love when deciding whom to wed. Love was a concern to them only *after* they wed—Artemis could see that plainly in the lines on their manicured hands—but whenever she touched on the subject, they pulled their hands away and said she was mistaken. Artemis was astonished.

Most of these people were married to one person but in love with another!

Is that what Orion expected would happen to him?

Artemis intended to ask him as soon as she could free herself. A half dozen people stood in a knot around her, waiting their turn to have their palms read. She did not want to rush through them; her work was too important. She might miss something.

She finished with the gentleman sitting before her and, stretching her sore back, called out to the stable boy on watch, "Will, please tell any who come now that I am too weary and need to rest."

No answer. Sunlight streamed across the straw-littered floor, and birdsong invited her outdoors. She rose and pulled her shawl about her shoulders. Perhaps she would take a walk if there were no more comers. "Will?"

"I have sent Will on his way," boomed a masculine voice from the doorway. The cluster of startled guests about her broke just enough for her to see the Earl of Lindenshire leaning with studied casualness against the frame of the stable door, his arms crossed. "I shall be happy to watch the door in his stead. For what—or for whom—am I to keep watch?"

It was plain to see Orion was less than happy, and the

guests who had already had their palms read and had been standing in clusters talking about the experience excused themselves rather quickly.

"Rats deserting a sinking ship," Artemis muttered.

With a nod, Orion dismissed the wide-eyed groom, who had peeked around the corner. It must have been clear their master wished to speak with Artemis alone, for the entire stable staff scurried away toward the inaudibility of the gray stone carriage house. Orion advanced upon her, his bearing stiff. He was dressed rather carelessly, his cravat wrinkled and tied loosely and his striped, parrot green waistcoat misbuttoned. *Stars and signs!* He was livid!

He stopped in front of her and planted his fists upon his hips, a shaft of light slashing over his golden brown hair and across his broad shoulders. She took a deep breath and steeled herself.

"I will not have my authority undermined. I can overlook many things—I *have* overlooked many things, by Jove!—but your encouraging my servants to skulk about and keep watch for me is beyond the limit, and if you do not care whether I am angry or not, perhaps you will have some compassion for young Will, whom I will be forced to dismiss if he displays such disloyalty again!"

"I . . . I am sorry," she said, genuinely contrite. "I had not thought of it that way. I meant no harm."

"And what," he asked tightly, "do you think you are doing out here?"

"Helping people."

"Helping people," he repeated. "Helping them like you helped my maid Maire?" He plunged on without waiting for an answer. "You advised her to accept the hand of a penniless farm laborer, when she might have a comfortable house and a husband with a pension."

"I can see why you might be a little peeved, but let me explain."

"Oh, by all means!" He sat on one of the upturned barrels. "I am all ears."

She frowned at his facetious manner. "Charles did tell Maire's father he was going to choose one of his daughters—"

"Precisely!"

"—but he will not choose Maire. He is going to ask for Maire's sister Catherine's hand instead."

"Because some swan caught a fish, you see fit to advise that girl to throw away her one chance at a secure future?"

"Would you have her throw away her one chance at love?"

"Love will not keep her dry in the rain or fill her belly."

"What good is being dry and sated if you've no one to love? Does love mean nothing to you? No," she answered her own question, "that cannot be, for I know you were happy for Miss Dove when you heard she'd eloped. 'Love is a delicacy,' you said then, 'and most get only the barest taste' . . ." Her voice trailed off as she put the pieces of the puzzle together. "Oh . . . yes. Yes, I understand now."

"I am ecstatic that one of us does."

A profound sympathy grew within her, and she didn't even try to keep it out of her words. "My poor Orion. You were deprived of your own feast," she said. "You were led to the table, given a taste, and then ejected from the banquet hall. I wondered how you could be so unlike the rest of them and yet so ridiculously similar in that one way."

"What are you talking about?" He affected a bored stance, examining his perfect manicure.

"You know very well what I am talking about."

He did not agree, but neither did he offer a denial. She went on, "You are still the same person I knew as a boy. Inside, you have not changed. You are unlike the rest of these"— she waved her hand in the direction of the house—"these tonnish people. You like bugs, but they do not notice them. You climb over the ruins and wonder at their origins, but they look at the ruins and wonder about the luncheon menu. And yet you are like them in one respect, Orion. You expect to marry where your heart will not go. Therefore, even though deep down you love me, you cannot believe we shall be wed. You cannot embrace your own destiny. And here I thought it was because you are stubborn!''

He affected a yawn. "This is a boring conversation."

"I know better. I have struck a sore spot, that is all. Elsewise, you would be sparring with me, as you usually do."

"We are getting nowhere."

"So it seems. You had better change the subject now, as you always do when I speak of destiny or of the signs."

He threw his hands into the air. "I need no encouragement for that!" He pinched his nose and then rubbed his forehead. "Listen to me, Artemis. What you do reflects upon me and my mother. You have no business reading my houseguest's palms."

"They already know I am a Gypsy . . . and they are my guests too, Orion."

"They are not truly your guests, and you know it."

"Yes, but *they* think they are."

His jaw flexed, and she knew he was barely keeping his temper in check. "While you are in my mother's employ," he said, "you will cease to indulge in your superstitious Gypsy nonsense. No signs, no tea leaves, no palm reading. Understand?"

"Perfectly."

"Good."

"What I understand is that you are being perfectly unreasonable."

"Unreasonable?"

"Illogical."

"Illogical!" He blustered. "You do not know the meaning of the word, silly girl."

"And you, Orion, do not see the signs. But that does not make you silly."

"Of course not!"

"Just ignorant."

His eyes smoldered with anger. "You are attempting to provoke me."

"Is it working?"

"No." He turned and walked away. "Remember my order, Artemis. No more Gypsy rubbish."

She watched him go. In spite of having deliberately provoked him, in spite of letting him think she didn't agree with him at all, she knew he was right about one thing. She shouldn't have read Lady Devonshire's palm. She hoped to bring Anna up within the confines of the Stonechase household. Though the servants would not look down their noses at her for employing her skills, she knew that the *ton*, in spite of their apparent fascination, would.

Artemis shook her head. She should be doing everything in her power to keep them from viewing her as anything but completely ordinary. Ah, but they already knew she'd been living as a Gypsy for the past sixteen years. She sighed and bent to pick up a piece of sweet, yellow straw. She was the granddaughter of an earl, by the signs. She had been born a lady, and, for Anna's sake, she could comport herself as any other lady did. If she did, the *ton* might overlook her years in caravan. Especially when she became the new Countess of Lindenshire.

*If* she became the new Countess of Lindenshire.

Orion's continued insistence that he would not marry her had begun to chip away at her confidence. He seemed adamant, his eyes cold and hard, whenever she mentioned it. Had she misinterpreted the signs? The owl, the star, and the ring around the moon? An idea had come to her a few nights ago, an idea she had at first rejected, but which good sense now told her she must ignore no longer.

Perhaps the signs had been pointing to their false betrothal and not to their eventual marriage at all.

A wave of despair threatened to overtake her, but she beat it down with her usual optimism. Even if the signs were pointing only to the false betrothal, that didn't mean she and Orion would not be wed. She had seen no signs indicating they would not be wed. And Orion did feel something for her.

But just what did he feel?

She knew he desired her physically. She knew he cared for her as a friend. But was there anything else? She didn't know. He had not said he loved her. Perhaps she should make plans, perhaps she should brace herself for the possibility that he did not love her and never would.

She sighed, knowing she could never prepare herself for that.

At least Anna would not suffer, though. Even if Artemis did not marry Orion, she would still have two thousand pounds and a position as Lady Lindenshire's companion. She was granddaughter to an earl. In time, she might be found socially acceptable, and then, of course, Anna would be, too. She had to look toward what was most important. It was imperative she appear no different from any other young lady.

And so for the next two days, she dressed with care, spoke softly, moved slowly and laughed but little, just like all of the other ladies.

And yet she *was* different. Where the ways of the *ton* were concerned, her education was incomplete. Because she knew nothing of fashion or of the personalities among the *ton*, she had little to add to the conversations of which she found herself a part. And since it was undoubtedly rude to ignore her, the ladies near her resorted to talking about Gypsies, a subject they thought they knew well and which they therefore viewed as common ground. But, inevitably, talk of Gypsies led to a request for a palm reading—which in turn caused Artemis to excuse herself on some pretext or other. It was most frustrating.

She soon reasoned that if she appeared to know something of their world, they would be less inclined to delve into hers. Perhaps all she had to do was to be able to mention Lady This or Lord That. The problem, of course, was that she knew nothing of the *ton* but what she'd learned at that miserable cyprians' ball, and that was the *last* thing she needed to mention.

Fortunately, the best teacher in all England also happened to be her fiancé.

"Excuse me, my lord," she said, quietly approaching him late in the day as he stood conversing with a small knot of gentlemen in the library. "A moment of your time, please?"

Orion excused himself and, taking her arm, led her to a private corner. He was dressed meticulously once more, his starched cravat tied perfectly and his silver embroidered black satin waistcoat buttoned properly under his expertly tailored gray coat. He executed a polite bow, and his golden brown eyes were gentle once more, yet wary, as he asked, "What do you need?"

"An education. I need an education." She explained what she had in mind. "And, while you are about it, there are a few other things that need attention before the betrothal ball." She explained how inept she'd been at the cyprians' ball with everything from introductions to dancing.

"I detest dancing." Orion looked grim. "But I agree that your plan is sound, and I commend you for thinking things through so thoroughly. Your reasoning is commendable. The best course of action *is* for you to blend in. Good for you."

"I will always be a Gypsy, Orion, and proudly, but Anna does not have to be."

"You sacrifice much."

"Not as much as you."

"I?"

"Well?" She threw him a mischievous smile. "You

*are* my new dancing master, and you detest dancing, remember?''

"Ah, yes." His lip curled. "A sacrifice indeed."

It was agreed they would meet in the Stonechase ballroom that night to practice. "Though I do not enjoy it," Orion said, "I am rather competent."

"I wager you are more than simply competent, Orion. Dancing must be an essential skill among the denizens of the London ballrooms. It cannot be fashionable to falter upon the dance floor. Therefore, it would surprise me if you were not quite skilled indeed."

"Perhaps," he said with a little shrug. "But however skilled I am, I cannot dance with you *and* assess your performance at the same time. For that, we will enlist the help of one of the guests, Mrs. Robertson."

"Mrs. Robertson?" Artemis said. "You cannot mean Mrs. Ophelia Robertson, the one who wears—"

Orion chuckled. "The very same."

Mrs. Robertson was a flamboyant and very wealthy old London hostess who favored bright greens, spangled oranges, purples, and yellows, which she often wore in outrageous combination. What came out of her mouth was usually just as outrageous as what she wore, and the *ton* was apparently fascinated with her. "Are you certain she is a suitable chaperone?" Artemis asked, deliberately dubious.

A smile crept about the edges of Orion's eyes. "Perfectly suitable." He lowered his voice. "Artemis, you must understand . . . Mrs. Robertson always comes away socially unscathed from episodes that would make a pariah of anyone else—such as what happened this past spring."

"Oh?"

He grinned. "She ran away to Gretna Green with a family servant."

Artemis raised her eyebrows. She might not know much about the *ton*, but she knew enough to collect how unusual such a thing was.

"Not to worry," Orion said, a warm smile on his face now. "She is an old friend of mine. She has my trust." He bowed. "If you'll excuse me?"

She nodded, and he returned to his group, leaving Artemis with a curiosity that gnawed at her the rest of the day.

Artemis had not yet spoken with Mrs. Robertson at length, though she had certainly noticed the old woman. One could not help but notice Ophelia Robertson. Her garish dress and outspoken manner made her the center of attention wherever she went. The rest of that day Artemis spent avoiding people, wandering far afield and wondering how two such different people as Mrs. Robertson and Orion Chase had formed what was evidently a tight friendship.

At Orion's request, the old woman was waiting for them both in the Stonechase ballroom that night. It was very late, even by Town hours, and the guests were all abed. Only a few candles had been lit so as to keep their presence in the ballroom secret.

As Artemis entered the vast room, the lone figure of one woman should not have been easily discernible. One woman should have been lost in the gloom, and yet Artemis's eyes found Mrs. Robertson immediately. A bark of delighted laughter well nigh escaped her. She couldn't have overlooked Mrs. Robertson if she'd tried, for she was dressed in a voluminous gown of spangled magenta and orange trimmed in pink feathers that matched the ones waving atop the massive turban that almost covered her white hair.

She moved forward and took Orion's hand familiarly. "I am so glad you asked for my help, my boy."

"Mrs. Robertson ... you have, of course, met my fiancée?" He motioned to Artemis.

"Pish-tosh!" the lady said. "Drop the formality, dear boy." She looked to Artemis. "Lindenshire and I got to know each other quite well this past summer." She patted Orion's hand. "Nasty business, that, but I see you have recuperated." She beamed at Artemis. "Of course we have been introduced, but I have not yet had the pleasure of speaking to this lovely creature at length. Well! Now we will remedy that pathetic state of affairs, will we not, my dear?"

Artemis dropped a curtsy. "Indeed, ma'am. I should like to get to know you better," she said, and she meant it. In spite of her flighty character, the old woman was obviously cunning and intelligent. Artemis decided she liked the plainspoken lady. But something the old woman had just said was nagging at her. "You and Orion met just this past summer?"

"That is so—though I feel as though I have known him much longer. Perhaps it is because he is so transparent," she said with a surreptitious wink.

"Transparent?" Orion said with a scowl.

Artemis giggled. "Oh, yes, Mrs. Robertson, he is transparent as a summer sky. Wears his heart on his sleeve."

"Hmmph." Orion held out his arm. "Shall we begin the dancing lessons, my dear—or are you two ladies not finished insulting me?"

"Well . . ." Artemis teased.

Mrs. Robertson cackled maliciously.

Orion heaved a long-suffering sigh, and Artemis laughed openly. "I hadn't imagined dancing lessons would be this much fun."

The lessons continued for four nights, with Mrs. Robertson serving as both chaperone and dance instructor. She was jolly, but she was also patient and kind, and Artemis knew Orion had been right to ask the old woman to help them. She seemed to knew even more of the latest *on-dits* than Orion, and she took great delight in educating Artemis, often in a shockingly forthright manner.

"Mrs. Robertson!" Orion cried, after she had offered a particularly juicy shred of gossip.

"Well?" Mrs. Robertson said. "We have no time to mince words."

"You never mince words."

"True." She dimpled. "True."

Artemis was glad. The outrageous old lady's version of events was probably more enlightening—and certainly more entertaining—than Orion's version would have been. Mrs. Robertson was a wealth of information, and Artemis was more confident about conversing with the house guests after only the first night spent under Ophelia Robertson's tutelage. Artemis was certain her dancing skills would be ready for the betrothal ball, too. She was so busy that the days melted away like snow in July, especially after Anna arrived three days later.

Artemis had been waiting impatiently in the front drawing room in anticipation of the coach's arrival. She had been passing the time sharing some Gypsy embroidery techniques with some of the ladies, who seemed to genuinely admire her skill with the needle. Artemis enjoyed embroidery, and she was quite good at it, but she simply could not keep her mind upon the work that day, and her eyes constantly strayed to the window.

As soon as she spotted the crested coach, she bid a hasty apology to her companions and flew from the room. How she had missed Anna! Her heart soared.

By the time she reached the driveway, the coach was stopped, and the nurse Lady Lindenshire had insisted upon hiring to fetch Anna had emerged. Lady Lindenshire, who had been strolling the lawn when the coach arrived, was nearing the coach.

"I am sorry, your ladyship," the nurse said, "the Gypsy woman refused to hand the child over to me, and I had no other choice than to bring her with me."

*Isabel?* Artemis's heart soared even higher. Isabel was a good friend, slightly older than Artemis, a widow who had no children of her own. Artemis had left Anna in her care, and she'd wondered if she'd ever see Isabel again.

"But she's been no trouble, in truth, and she treats the little one well, I must say," the nurse said. "Still, I apologize for bringing her. You'll have to put her up and send her back. You can take the funds from my wages, if you wish."

"It does not signify, Miss Bull," the countess assured her. "I am still glad you were there, and I appreciate Miss Isabel's loyalty to the baby. Now, where is the little darling?" She looked over the nurse's shoulder and into the closed carriage, from which Isabel was carefully attempting to extract a sleeping Anna without disturbing her.

Artemis touched the countess's shoulder, and the two traded fond looks of excited anticipation.

"Oh, Artemis, my dear . . . you must be overset with happiness."

Artemis nodded and stepped up to the coach.

Isabel emerged and greeted her with a kiss and whispered, "She just got to sleep. She was up most of last night, and"— her eyes grew wide—"and look at you!"

Her gaze swept Artemis from head to toe, taking in the fine blue muslin gown with its low neckline, long embroidered sleeves, and fancy satin sash. Gone were the worn boots and scarves. Isabel's eyes lit upon the delicate kid slippers and the strand of pearls at Artemis's neck, and she whispered, "I had no idea, my lady . . ."

"Now, stop that this instant," Artemis said. "I am the same as I ever was."

Isabel shook her head. "Yes, but now you look the part."

Artemis wrinkled her brow and was trying to interpret the remark when Orion emerged from the house.

"Is that him?" Isabel whispered, her eyes flicking toward Orion.

"Yes," Artemis said, her heart swelling with a pride she couldn't have contained if she'd tried. "He is my betrothed." *At least for now,* she added to herself. And then the enormity of the moment washed over Artemis as she realized Orion was about to have his first glimpse of the little girl he could soon be rearing as his daughter.

She held her breath and watched as he approached—and then she exhaled forcefully as she saw that every window in Stonechase Manor was lined with faces silently peering toward them, waiting to see what would happen. She was not the only one who was eager to witness Orion's first look at the baby.

Orion smiled as he neared, and his mama fell into step beside him.

"This is our Anna, then."

*Our* Anna. Artemis quivered. The warmth in his voice seemed genuine.

He moved the blanket aside and, as he studied Anna's face, a gentle smile softened his features. He blinked and tipped his head. And then, to Artemis's astonishment, he pulled out his spectacles and slipped them on for a moment before tucking them back into his pocket. "Lovely child," he said. "She looks much like you, Artemis."

Lady Lindenshire beamed, and Isabel raised an eyebrow.

"Thank you, my lord," Artemis said with delight. "I shall take that as a compliment."

"It was meant to be." He turned to the two nurses. "You must be Nurse Bull and Miss Isabel. You both come highly recommended."

"My lord," they said in unison. Nurse Bull executed a polite curtsy, and beside her, Isabel attempted the same.

Orion smiled. "Thank you for taking such good care of our Anna," he said. "I am certain both of you were much needed. She looks like she could be a bundle of mischief—like her big sister."

Everyone laughed. The countess patted him on the back, the nurse looked relieved, and Isabel positively worshipped Orion with her eyes. Artemis imagined Isabel had felt quite put out when Nurse Bull had shown up demanding Anna. Orion was clearly doing his best to make Isabel feel less superfluous, and Artemis could have kissed him for it, right then and there.

"Come," he said, "Nurse Bull and Miss Isabel must be very tired. We shall show them to the nursery and send up a meal and hot water."

"Thank you, my lord," the nurse and Isabel said together.

Artemis took the baby and fell into step between Orion and his mama. Anna's familiar weight felt good in her arms, and she bent to breathe in the perfume of her soft skin. Isabel and the nurse, who, in spite of their disagreement over who should look after Anna, had clearly formed a friendship, lagged behind, gathering their and Anna's things from the coach.

"Orion," Artemis whispered, "the guests are all staring at us from the windows."

"Searching for resemblances. What color eyes does Anna have?"

"Light blue, like mine," Artemis said.

He raised one eyebrow and gave a small shrug. "Let them look, then." Her eyes looked nothing like his, and neither did Anna's head of curly black hair or pale, milky white skin. "After Anna wakes up," he said, "we will be sure to make ourselves available for a closer inspection. I am certain the guests will avail themselves of the opportunity soon enough."

They did.

For two days, the three of them—Artemis, Orion, and Anna—picnicked on the lawn or strolled the gardens or capered through the house and, as the two adults watched Anna experiment happily with the piano keys, chase blue butterflies, or stamp her tiny foot on the crisp autumn leaves, the fifty house guests hovered nearby, trying not to look obvious, before approaching in ones and twos.

They stayed just long enough to compare the baby's features to Orion's and then left, some clearly relieved, and some clearly disappointed. Artemis and Orion shared more than one moment of near disaster as their eyes met and they were hard-pressed to hold in their laughter.

Old Countess Rangnor took one look and walked away muttering. She was quite hard of hearing and had a habit of talking loudly to herself. Her private thoughts were often not very private. "Demmed boring house party, if you ask me," she said.

Artemis and Orion didn't even have a go at curbing their laughter.

The inspection lasted for two days. For two days, Artemis had such a lovely time with Anna and Orion that she hardly thought about the signs, and no one asked her to read palms or tea leaves. Thus, it was quite easy to satisfy her resolve to fit in—and to follow Orion's order to restrain herself from using her Gypsy talents—until the second night after Anna's arrival, the night of their betrothal ball.

# CHAPTER ELEVEN

Orion gave Artemis a satisfied nod as their eyes met across the ballroom floor. A smile flashed in her clear blue eyes, and then she returned her gaze to her dancing partner, the Marquis of Blackshire, a man Orion admired greatly.

Orion shook his head, marveling at the change in Artemis, at how genuine her transformation seemed. She hadn't stumbled the entire evening, either at the dance or at the social graces. Elegantly gowned in snowy white muslin, she wore her hair up and a red rose tucked behind one ear. She was behaving exactly as a lady should—as she had been all week.

Orion frowned, feeling guilty for having rebuked her so harshly for the palm reading nonsense. He should have talked with her, not handed down an edict as though she were feather-brained. Orion knew she wasn't.

In spite of her belief in all of that superstitious Gypsy rubbish, Artemis was intelligent. That palm reading business had been his own fault, in truth. He should have anticipated that, with nothing else to talk about, she'd have had no way of avoiding such nonsense. If he'd thought to arm her with a little gossip and a few names to drop, the palm reading never would have come up. Yes, it was all his fault. Artemis was a pleasant and reasonable young lady.

In fact, he had been content to pass time in her company this past week. They had spent long hours together as he'd taught her the dancing and other social intricacies and oddities she needed to know. He watched her now as she smiled up at the tall marquis, her expression neatly hiding the concentration Orion knew must be lurking behind her carefully pleasant expression. He was proud of her, by Jove!

Ophelia Robertson appeared like a wraith at his elbow, gowned and turbaned in magenta and yellow spangled silk. She nodded toward Artemis. "She is trying so hard to please you."

The comment begged a response. Mrs. Robertson was one of only three people who knew what he'd been through three months ago. She'd been kind to him then, and she'd earned his trust. A part of him longed to confide in her now, and yet he could not. His secrets were also Artemis's secrets, and he would not betray her confidence.

"I cannot thank you enough for helping us these past several nights," he said. "I do not know what we should have done without you to serve as chaperone and critical eye."

Mrs. Robertson smiled. "Fortunately, my taste in dancing is better than my taste in clothing, eh, my boy?" She cackled. "But I daresay you did not need my critical eye." She waved her purple silk fan toward Artemis. "I vow she has more natural grace in her than any other young lady of my acquaintance. All she needed was someone to show her the steps. Nothing you or I said could improve upon how she executed them, and you know it."

He tipped his head to the side and looked at Artemis.

"She does cut a rather fine dash," he said as he watched her weave in and out of the two lines of dancers opposite the dashing Marquis of Blackshire. "They look well together," he said.

"Good thing Blackshire is married, eh?"

"Mmm . . ." Orion gave a noncommittal nod and glanced down at Mrs. Robertson, who was staring at him with a smug expression. "What?" he asked.

"You are in love with her."

"Of course I am in love with her," he lied. "We are to be wed."

He wondered if the shrewd dear had somehow guessed that the betrothal was a sham, and he worried that she might attempt to play matchmaker—with disastrous results—but the old trickster said nothing more. Instead, she merely tapped his arm with her fan and, with a smile, disappeared into the card room moments later.

Orion relaxed. Everything was going as it should. Still, the most logical and prudent thing to do was to warn Artemis that Mrs. Robertson might have caught wind of the truth, so, when the dance ended, he led her from the floor himself.

"It is warm inside, my dear. Let us take some air." He steered her toward the tall glass terrace doors.

"Oh, but I am not overwarm."

"You are flushed," he insisted.

"I do not feel so, and I have promised the next dance to the Viscount Trowbridge."

"Trowbridge," he said, trying to keep the bitterness he felt for the viscount out of his voice, "will have to wait. I wish to speak with you." He pulled her through the doors and over to a more private, yet still visible spot near the low stone wall that enclosed the high terrace. The moon was just past full, and the scent of the faded autumn foliage wafted up from the dim garden far below.

"Having fun, my dear?" he asked.

"Yes. And what is so important that you must drag me out here? And since when do you call me 'my dear'?"

He shifted so only she could see his face. "Since when? Since you resisted my efforts to bring you out here quietly . . . and since the entire ballroom is now staring at us . . . and since I would wager there are among them one or two at least who can read lips." He moved closer to her and lowered his face over hers.

"What are you doing?"

"They think we are quarreling. I am changing their minds." He stole a quick kiss, pressing his lips against hers for the briefest of moments. Her blue eyes registered shock.

He chanced a glimpse into the ballroom, where his guests' expressions showed only mild surprise before the vast majority of them turned away, disappointed again. Yet if they'd been able to see Artemis's face, they would have been satisfied enough, for as he broke the kiss, she opened eyes heavy-lidded with desire. He stepped away.

Hell and blast, why had he kissed her, of all things? He was not given to spontaneity. He was attracted to her, but kissing her? He knew better. Didn't he?

He did.

"I am a fool," he said. "I should not have kissed you again. An ardent pressing of my lips to the back of your hand would have served. I panicked."

"I did not mind," she said with a smile that was not shy enough for his liking.

"You have half convinced yourself you are in love with me."

"I do love you, Orion."

"As a brother," he said. "We were born on the same day. We grew up together. We are like twins. You love me as a brother, not as a beau, and certainly not as a husband."

Grinning, she stepped past him and headed back inside. "Think what you will, Orion, but what will be will be." She glanced back and tossed over her shoulder, "And I do love you—exactly as I should. I always have."

She slipped back into the ballroom and disappeared among the crowd.

"What the devil did she mean by that?" he muttered, though he was afraid he knew exactly what she meant. "Silly chit," he said to no one in particular as he watched her pass through the ballroom doors.

"Is it so difficult to believe she might truly love you, my boy?" asked a voice far below.

Orion leaned over the low wall and peered into the darkness. Ophelia Robertson was grinning up at him, illumined with moonlight and the faint orange light from the terrace flambeaux.

She held up one finger. "Wait there," she said and made for the sweep of the wide terrace stairs. She climbed them more nimbly than her years would lead most to suspect she was capable. Orion wasn't surprised, however. He had come to expect from her the unexpected, and the longer he knew Mrs. Robertson, the less she surprised him. She wasn't the least out of breath as she gained his side.

"Why should your betrothed not be in love with you?"

How long she had been down there in the shadows Orion didn't know, but if she'd been there longer than a few moments, she might have heard enough of his conversation with Artemis to collect that their engagement was false. He decided to answer her with truth— just not the *whole* truth.

"She cannot have formed any true feelings. She has known me as an adult for only a little over a month."

"You knew Marianna Grantham for only a fortnight," Mrs. Robertson answered.

"That was different." *She* was different. Steady, logical Marianna Grantham was as different from Artemis Rose as spiders were from octopi. They both had the same number of legs, but that's where the similarity ended.

"Different?" Mrs. Robertson mused. "In some ways,

yes, but in others . . . well, I suspect the differences are not as great as you would like them to be.''

"Dare I ask what you mean?"

She gave a sly smile and patted his hand. "You will figure it out sooner or later, I think. But do not stay out here pondering my words too long, my boy. Supper will be announced soon. You would not wish to miss dancing the de Coverley with your betrothed at your very own betrothal ball. Would you?" She cackled and set off for the ballroom.

She knew. He would wager his best microscope on it.

Ophelia seated herself unobtrusively next to a potted, trellised red rose to await the de Coverley, which would be quite a show, she thought. The Sir Roger de Coverley was always the last dance of any formal evening, announced right before supper, and Lindenshire was dreading it, she knew, for all eyes would be upon him and his Gypsy. Especially after the dance ended. That is when he would formally announce the betrothal—and he would have to show some definite sign of affection for Miss Rose. Ophelia wondered how the dear, mixed-up boy was going to handle that.

Not far away from her sat a group of six young people she knew quite well. There were Lord and Lady Blackshire, Lord and Lady Trowbridge, Lady Jane Tregally, and the Honorable Miss Lydia Grantham. They were talking and laughing animatedly with Miss Rose, whom they had drawn into their circle and held there. The only one missing was Lindenshire, but Ophelia knew better than to hope he would join them.

Truesdale Sinclair, the Viscount Trowbridge, was a part of the group, after all.

Unbeknownst to all but a few, Truesdale was Ophelia's own son. He was a good man, a fine man, loyal and intelligent and quite popular among the *ton*—yet Lindenshire avoided him. The reason was Marianna Sinclair, née Grantham. She was True's new bride, but she was also the lady Lindenshire had fallen disastrously in love with almost three months before.

There was no animosity between the two men. On the contrary, Lindenshire had invited Marianna and Truesdale to the house party and betrothal ball and then welcomed them with genuine warmth. But Lindenshire had also kept his distance.

It was a shame, for the young people had been having a grand time together all week. Ophelia looked upon the two couples in the group with satisfaction. She'd had a hand in bringing both pairs together. Their marriages were as sound and as happy as her own, and she just knew she could do the same for Lindenshire and his little Gypsy. They were meant for each other. They were in love. Miss Rose knew it. Blast, any simpleton could see it. Why couldn't the brilliant Lindenshire?

She chuckled to herself. It was no matter. All she had to do was find a way to keep them together long enough for *both* of them to realize it.

Ophelia's hearing was exquisite, and she used it to good advantage. She'd overheard more than one interesting snippet of conversation this week, and she'd been able to put other little bits and pieces together. She knew very well Lindenshire's engagement to Miss Rose was fake, and she would bet her best turban it would be broken before the last departing houseguest's carriage rolled off the grounds if she didn't do something about it.

And that would be a shame. No, it simply would not do!

Lindenshire thought he had her figured out, tamed, and under control, but he still underestimated her, the pup. How she was going to enjoy helping Artemis Rose turn his ordered, logical little world on end!

And, unless she missed her guess, there was one other

match to be made at Stonechase . . . a match not unlike her own. She smiled behind her fan.

Supper was announced and Lindenshire came inside, tugging on his gloves just in time to take his place opposite Artemis in the set for the Sir Roger de Coverley. But just as the music started, a commotion was heard at the other side of the room, and a shiny head of dark curls burst forth from a barrier of long skirts.

"Armis!" the tiny girl cried and toddled across the polished wooden floor toward her big sister. At close to a year old, Anna had just learned to walk. Though she stumbled a half dozen times on her way over to Miss Rose, she persisted with a look of complete concentration on her little face—and a corresponding expression of joy when she made it to the safety of her big sister's outstretched arms.

"Anna, darling! What are you doing downstairs at this time of the night?"

"I am sorry, ma'am," the nurse said, scurrying forward. "She wouldn't sleep, so I took her to the kitchen for a warm posset of milk, and she got away from me. Attracted to the light and the music, she was. I'll just take her back with me now. Come now, little one. Let us leave the party to the adults."

To Ophelia's surprise, Lindenshire stepped forward. "I see no need to disappoint her, Nurse." He nodded to the orchestra. "A waltz for my sister-to-be, please!" Scooping the baby into his arms, he pulled Miss Rose right up alongside them, and as the waltz began, the three of them twirled across the floor by themselves. Miss Rose beamed, baby Anna laughed and clapped her hands, and everyone on the periphery smiled. The waltz ended, and the company applauded—which elicited more clapping from Anna, and everyone laughed.

Ophelia shook her head in wonder. Lindenshire was clever. Too clever. The dear, dratted boy had found a way to divert the guests' attention from himself and Miss Rose to the adorable moppet. It was a brilliant maneuver, and Ophelia would have loved to pinch his little neck.

Peabody cleared his throat. "The soup will be getting cold, my lord."

"The Sir Roger de Coverley!" Lindenshire said with a nod.

The song began and, as he attempted to hand Anna over to the nurse, the baby cried and clung to his shoulder.

"Do carry her upstairs, Orion," Miss Rose said.

"I will miss the de Coverley," he warned.

Ophelia chuckled to herself, knowing very well he did not want to dance the de Coverley in the first place.

"There will be other balls," his betrothed said with a shrug and a lift of one delicate black eyebrow.

"Indeed," Lindenshire said a little too tightly as he strode from the ballroom.

Ophelia chuckled again as the Gypsy gel watched Lindenshire go. The chit had love in her eyes and not a doubt or worry in her superstitious, spontaneous, fun-loving mind. The gel was obviously quite certain Fate would take matters into hand, that Lindenshire would come to realize he loved her.

But Ophelia knew better.

The boy had fallen in love instantly the first time, to his utter detriment. He'd had his poor heart broken. He wasn't going to make the same mistake again. He had told himself he was not in love with his Artemis, that they hadn't known each other long enough for love to blossom, but the dear silly boy hadn't taken their first eight years together into account.

He was right, in a way. The two of them *hadn't* fallen in love these past five weeks. No, they had fallen in love as children.

Ophelia gave a sly smile. No doubt the boy was grateful to have dodged the de Coverley bullet. If he dawdled long enough in the nursery, he would miss their formal announcement and parading into the dining room for supper, too.

She pursed her lips. Only someone as clever as Lindenshire could avoid his own betrothed while still appearing solicitous. And if he were allowed to keep that up, their engagement would be broken within a day or two.

She had to do something.

Artemis was seated next to an old, white-haired duke who fell asleep during the first course. The poor dear snored through the turtle soup, the baked sturgeon, and the roast partridge, with everyone attempting to pretend he was awake. At last, Artemis caught the eye of the young lady on the other side of the duke just as a particularly loud sound emanated from his open mouth. Her name was Lady Cassandra Something-Or-Other—Artemis could not remember what—and she was thin and willowy and nondescript. Terribly homely, with crooked features and mouse-brown hair, the milk-and-water miss had been well nigh transparent since the house party began, spending most of her time hiding behind her rotund mama—a countess friend of Lady Lindenshire's and someone with a fair amount of influence within Society, as Artemis understood it, though one couldn't have predicted it from looking at the woman's wispy daughter.

Artemis was surprised and delighted to see a spark of mirthy mischief in the girl's eyes, and she winked at her and flicked a glance at the duke. The girl gave a shy but conspiratorial smile.

"I find balls deadly dull, too," Artemis whispered.

"Oh, indeed," the girl whispered back, cleverly catching onto Artemis's game immediately. "Balls are almost as boring as desserts." To punctuate the point, she dipped her spoon into the rich cherry custard before her and popped it into her mouth with obvious relish.

Artemis chortled. "I would sleep, too, if I could."

Lady Cassandra nodded. "Oh, yes"—she molded her features into a look of mock sympathy—"but I suppose it would be impolite to do so at one's betrothal ball."

Artemis sighed quietly but dramatically. "Yes, I suppose."

They chuckled quietly together and then began talking without interruption as though they had known each other for a lifetime. After the fifth course, the duke nearly fell off his chair. It was not, apparently, an unexpected turn of events, for two burly footmen stationed behind the duke's chair rushed forward before the gentleman could slump against Artemis.

"Paul, Selwin," Lady Lindenshire ordered, "escort His Grace to his bedchamber, please." The pair of footmen gently complied, carrying the duke more than escorting him. A third footman removed the duke's chair and table setting, a fourth and fifth moved Artemis and Cassandra's chairs closer together, and supper went on without a wrinkle.

So did the two young ladies' conversation.

Seated as they now were, with extra space between them and the other diners and less space between them than before the duke's departure, they were close enough together for Cassandra to share confidences— and share them she did. The young lady was sharp-set for a sympathetic friend, someone close to her own age, and once she started talking, it was as though a river had overflowed its banks.

Artemis learned that Cassandra's mother hardly ever let her youngest daughter out of her sight. It was her mother's intention for Cassandra never to wed. All of her older sisters had married well, but Cassandra's destiny—or so her mother had deemed it—was to persist in the single state into spinsterhood so she could keep her aging parents company and dote on them until they passed on, at which time Cassandra would inherit one of the family's cottages as compensation. She should be grateful for such an arrangement, her parents thought.

Cassandra had other ideas, however.

She was in love. In love with a young man who lived near one of her parents' two estates. A country farmer, he had inherited his father's land and was doing quite well for himself.

"I adore him," Cassandra confessed, but then she frowned.

"Why the sad face, then?"

"Because I do not know if he shares my feelings. He might . . . at least I think he might. I see him at church each Sunday and we"—she glanced at her mother surreptitiously—"we spoke twice in front of the vicar before my mother put a stop to it."

She lowered her voice to a whisper. "And he winks at me every Sunday! He asked me to dance at our last assembly, but, as my mother will not allow me to dance with a gentleman, let alone speak with one, I do not know his true mind, nor do I have any chance of discovering it." Her eyes misted over.

"I can help you," Artemis said before she considered her words.

"You can? Oh! Oh, I confess I was hoping you could!" In her excitement, her voice had become quite loud. "I heard about—"

Artemis flicked her eyes at Orion, pressed her lips together, and held up one finger. Cassandra fell silent and ate another bite of ice.

"Be patient for a moment," Artemis whispered. Glancing up the table, she saw that Orion was in deep discussion with the Marquis of Blackshire. *Good.* Signaling to a footman, she asked for Lady Cassandra to be brought a cup of tea. "With plenty of leaf," she requested quietly with a wink.

The footman understood. He had asked her two days ago if a move to London was in his future, for he did not wish to marry in the country only to be separated from his bride. The leaves had said he would stay in the country, and the footman was now happily on the lookout for a wife here near Stonechase. He delivered the tea with an answering wink. Cassandra drank it and nudged it over to Artemis, wide-eyed.

Artemis waited for a spirited conversation to erupt at the other end of the table before she chanced peering down into the cup.

Usually, the leaves were unclear, but this time, unfortunately, their message was unmistakable. Her heart ached for her new friend, and she dreaded telling her the news.

"Well?" Lady Cassandra prompted eagerly. "What do the leaves tell you?"

"He cares for you," Artemis said gently, "but he does not love you."

"What?!"

"That does not mean," Artemis added hastily, "that he will not *come* to love you. You may simply need more time together to—"

Her end of her sentence was drowned in the heart-rending sobs that welled forth from Lady Cassandra. The entire company froze, and every pair of eyes fixed upon the girl—every pair but Orion's. They were fixed on the empty teacup, and he was frowning.

He knew.

"Cassandra!" the girl's mother screeched. "Whatever is the matter?"

"H-he d-does not love me! She read the leaves, and he—he does not love me!" Cassandra wailed and fled the room.

Orion watched, horrified. Every member of the company knew exactly who "she" was—and they were all staring at her with varying expressions of amusement, derision, distaste, or pity. He felt as though he were caught beneath a swarm of descending locusts and knew full well he could do nothing to escape them.

"My apologies, my lord," Cassandra's mama said to

Orion. "I beg your pardon. My daughter has only just come out, and—"

"She is twenty-one," Artemis said, "and most girls her age have been out for two or three years."

The woman was clearly put to the blush. "Her father and I did not think it prudent to—"

"To allow her to fall in love with a man and marry? To have her own home and her own children to care for?"

"She is not in love with a man!"

"No, but she could be, if you would allow her to venture from behind your skirts!" Artemis answered. "If you would allow her to speak with this young man she loves, they would be betrothed within a week." She tipped the teacup forward. "It is all right here, as plain as the sun."

*"Enough!"* Orion roared. Appalled, embarrassed, and frustrated, he was as shocked as the rest of the company to hear his own tone of voice, but he couldn't have moderated it if he had tried—which he didn't. She had gone too far.

Telling futures at the table, of all things! Making the poor chit cry! And ringing a peal over the girl's mother and criticizing her parental decisions! The guests would find it all more delicious than anything else they tasted that night. They'd never forget it.

The past week had been perfect. If she'd continued behaving as a lady, they'd have forgotten she'd ever had anything to do with the Gypsies, but now, Orion knew, they'd never forget. She would be a Gypsy in their minds forever more.

And Orion would never live it down. Hell and blast, *Anna* would never live it down. Especially not since he'd let his temper boil over and shouted at Artemis at the blasted supper table.

"Palms and tea leaves!" he thundered. "Superstitious rubbish! There is nothing in that cup but some desic-cated, macerated plant matter!"

All movement had ceased. The guests stared. Let them, Orion thought sourly. He couldn't turn back the clock and keep Artemis from making a spectacle, and, at this point, he could do no worse than to show how flamingly displeased he was.

Artemis kit her brows stubbornly together. "There is truth in this cup, Orion, future truth."

"This man you speak of is in that cup?" he asked evenly.

"Yes."

"And Lady Cassandra?"

Artemis nodded.

"And their entire future?"

"One possible future," she said, casting a baleful glance at Cassandra's mother, "yes."

Orion pounded on the table, making the silver dance. "Lady Cassandra is slight and lithe, to be sure, but she will not fit in that cup!"

Someone tittered.

Artemis wrinkled her brow. "You jest, my lord. Your argument is ridiculous."

"Granted!" Orion cried. "It is just as ridiculous as your assertion that you can predict whether the gentleman in question will ask Lady Cassandra to marry him."

"But I *can* predict that, with a certainty. You have only to look into the cup and you will see—"

He held up his palm and pointed to it with his other hand. "I see nothing but lines here, and in that cup I see nothing but a smear of wet leaves. Do you see something different?"

"No," she answered. "In truth, I see exactly what you see—"

"Aha!"

"—but I interpret what I see differently. I could teach you to see clearly, too, Orion."

"To see clearly?" He scoffed. "You would teach me to deceive myself as you do yourself."

"The only thing I have deluded myself about is you, my lord."

"Me?"

"I thought you would come to see reason."

"Reason?"

"Logic."

"Logic?" Orion seethed. How dare she publicly question his capacity to reason? How dare she publicly malign him? She had gone over the edge.

And then, in his anger, Orion went over the edge himself. Way over the edge.

"Logic, hmmph! You, Gypsy, do not know the meaning of the word. You are stupid if you think you can pair logic with superstition!"

"It seems," Lady Devonshire interjected, "that the two of you already have, Lindenshire."

The supper guests laughed nervously.

Orion came to his senses and caught hold of his rampaging temper. Blast! Had he just called Artemis stupid? He shouldn't have done that. It only made his maddening mull worse. Everyone was waiting expectantly for the next volley, their eyes shifting from him to Artemis and back.

Suddenly, Orion knew what he had to do.

Their sham engagement had fulfilled its purpose. There wasn't a single member of the *ton* who would still believe Artemis had been Orion's mistress. They could end their engagement any time, and if he ended it right there and then, during their shockingly public argument, there would be no lingering doubt as to why the betrothal had been broken.

# CHAPTER TWELVE

Ophelia watched Lindenshire's face, watched uncertainty give way to reason and finally to resolve. He squared his shoulders and turned to his betrothed.

"Miss Rose," he said, "we will never agree. It is foolish of us to think we might—"

"Of course it is, my boy!" Ophelia stood up quickly, giving her head a toss. She felt the enormous orange feathers atop her head wave precipitously. She had everyone's attention. She took a deep breath, stalling for time. She had to think of something in a trice! "It . . . it is foolish to go on arguing like this. It is no way for a betrothed couple to behave—and certainly no way for a newlywed couple to find happiness."

"Indeed," Lindenshire said, "which is why I am afraid we—"

"I have a solution!" Ophelia blurted, an idea coming to her. "Since Miss Rose believes in her . . . her methods as fervently as you do in your logic, I propose a contest."

"A contest?" Lady Devonshire asked.

"Yes, my dear Elizabeth, a contest. A wager, actually. A wager to settle the matter."

"A wager!" Lady Devonshire cried. "Capital idea. Who will wager what?"

Ophelia turned to Miss Rose. "My dear Miss Rose, can you predict with any certainty the major events that will happen to people within a large group—even as many as thousands?"

"I . . . I suppose I could."

"Would you use palms, the leaves, the signs?"

"I am not certain," Miss Rose said. "I have never been asked to make such a far-reaching set of predictions. With that many people, there would be many factors involved. I suppose if I had time, I would probably use a combination of all three."

"Not that it would help," Lindenshire scoffed and scowled.

The little Gypsy planted her hands upon her hips and scowled right back at him. "Those things helped when I predicted Mary Wilson, the parlor maid, would fall and injure herself."

"She was waxing the floor!" Lindenshire cried.

"I predicted one of our guests would come down sick."

"There are well nigh fifty guests. With this changeable weather, of *course* one of them would come down sick."

"I predicted the sheep would be lost."

Lindenshire shook his head. "My shepherd has just lost his best dog, and the flock is in chaos. Can you not see anyone could have made the same predictions just by observing the situations and using logic to predict what would happen?"

"If that is so, Lord Logic, why did *you* not predict those misfortunes and move to prevent them?"

"*Lord Logic?*" Lady Devonshire chortled. Laughter erupted here and there among the rest of the diners.

Lindenshire scowled even harder. "Logic is certainly more reliable than superstition."

Ophelia laughed. "Then you believe you could better

your lovely fiancée's predictions by applying logic to your assessment of the facts?"

"I do," said the earl.

"Well then"—she licked her lips—"I propose Lord Lindenshire and Miss Rose should solve their impasse with a wager: to see which of them can most closely predict how many couples among the *ton* will become betrothed by the eve of the new year."

Lindenshire balked, as Ophelia knew he would. The stubborn boy had been about to end their engagement then and there, Ophelia was certain.

"It is an unfair wager," he said, "for I am intimately connected with the subjects, whereas m—"

Clearly, he'd been about to say *my fiancée* but had caught himself in time. He was clever and quick, and he still was not caught irrevocably in the web Ophelia was weaving. She couldn't let him wiggle free.

"—whereas *Miss Rose*," he continued, "is new to society. She cannot possibly be expected to be able to make such a prediction without knowing—"

"I do not need facts, my lord," Miss Rose said. "I have the signs. They will guide me, as they always have." She looked to Ophelia and lifted her chin. "I agree to the wager, madam, unless . . ."

"Unless?" Ophelia prompted.

"Unless my logical fiancé is too timid . . . too afraid to pit his skills against mine." She turned her defiant gaze to Lindenshire, who showed no reaction.

*Oh, well done!* Ophelia silently congratulated Miss Rose. *You have him now, my gel!* Somehow, Ophelia managed to hide her glee.

Seconds ticked by as the two of them locked gazes, facing each other down. Not a single guest moved. Ophelia wondered with amusement if most of them were even breathing, hanging on to the moment as they were, waiting to hear what Lindenshire would say in answer.

"I accept the wager," he finally said. "Making such

a prediction is a simple matter of paying close attention to the facts.''

Miss Rose shook her head. "Making such a prediction is a simple matter of paying close attention to the signs.''

"Well, then,'' Ophelia said and clapped her hands together with satisfied amusement. "You both have exactly twenty-four hours to make your predictions and seal them into envelopes. I will hold the envelopes and open them publicly at a ball.''

"What ball?'' Lady Devonshire asked.

"A grand ball to be given in our principles' honor by me two days after Epiphany.''

There erupted among the supper guests a swell of excited murmurs. Ophelia was known for her balls, for she always concocted some outrageous happening to spring upon her guests when they least expected it. Invitations to her affairs were fiercely vied for, and speculation about what sort of spectacle she would create was always the talk of breakfast tables across London for weeks beforehand.

"What are the stakes?'' Lady Devonshire asked suddenly.

"Oh . . .'' Ophelia said with a sly smile, "I fancy we should allow the two lovebirds to decide the stakes between them later,'' she said with a suggestive wink at Lindenshire, to the amusement of the guests.

He met her gaze frankly, starkly. She took a most naughty pleasure from the look that passed between them. He knew he'd been outfoxed, though the poor boy hadn't the first notion why she'd done it.

The truth was, there was more than one reason.

The most important, of course, was that Artemis Rose and Orion Chase were meant for each other. That was plain to see. Or it was to Ophelia. She seemed to be able to see such things where others could not.

She had known the Blackshires were right for each other, and her son True and his new bride, the lady Orion had fallen in love with only three months ago—

or thought he had. Orion had been fascinated by her, to be sure, but he was not arse-over-instep in love with her, as he was with the little Gypsy gel. He was passionately, madly in love with *her*. He just needed time to realize just how deeply in love he really was.

And now, thanks to the wager she had orchestrated, the falsely betrothed couple would have to stay together at least another three weeks.

She smiled and smacked her lips all through the rest of supper. Yes, everything would work out famously. Lindenshire and Miss Rose would wed, and Marianna and Miss Rose would become friends. Marianna was a girl fashioned after Ophelia's own outrageous heart. Rebellious, spontaneous, she needed a bosom friend, someone more like herself than the other simpering, mincing matrons of her social set, and Artemis Rose would do just fine. She gave a happy sigh.

Perhaps even Lindenshire and True would become friends. She was sure that, as soon as Lindenshire collected that Marianna could not hold a candle to the little Gypsy in his affections, he would forgive True for Marianna's falling in love with True instead of himself. She just knew the two of them could be great friends.

The dear boys!

# CHAPTER THIRTEEN

The day dawned rainy and drear, but Artemis awakened with a sense of excitement, as though spring were just around the corner instead of weeks away. In spite of having slept only a few hours, she rose and dressed with care, then tiptoed into the silent nursery.

Anna lay sleeping with her knees tucked under her and her backside pointed into the air, a favorite rag doll their mother had made for her clutched tightly to her shoulder. Nurse Bull was in her adjoining room—asleep, judging from the loud rasping snores emanating from within—and Isabel was asleep, too, curled up on a small bed near Anna's cot.

Artemis added a blanket to Isabel's bed, then snugged the covers over Anna and pressed a quick kiss to the baby's sweet-smelling forehead before creeping back out into the hall.

After a quick breakfast of warm, sweet bread and fresh milk taken in the kitchen, she wrapped a pair of shawls about her shoulders and quit the house in spite of the misting rain. She had less than twenty-four hours to make an accurate prediction, and the signs weren't going to appear if she were cooped up in some drawing room embroidering all day. And who knew when the rain would end? She stepped out into the drizzly December morning, her mind open and her confidence high. What she needed was to ramble across the grounds with an open mind, heart, and eyes.

An hour later, her ramblings had yielded some promising signs.

It had occurred to her she ought to look for pairs of things, and not just any old pairs would do. A pair of shoes would not do. Too common. But the pair of twin black lambs born a week early during the night weren't. There were some people within the *ton* with the last name of Lamb, she thought, and she was certain the unusual birth signified a betrothal among them.

Two dead fish—she wrinkled her nose and walked on. Two distant thunderclaps, close together. A pair of leaves hanging next to each other on an otherwise barren tree. All good.

And then there were the two beehives.

As Artemis strolled the barren pear orchard, the beekeeper, perched on a stool to replenish the hives' winter supply of sugared rosewater, lost his balance. He wasn't hurt, thank goodness, but he fell heavily against one hive, which toppled and took its neighbor along with it. The sleepy bees were suddenly everywhere.

The beekeeper, from within his protective shroud, shouted, "Run, Miss Artemis!" and she did.

She'd been badly stung once as a child, when she'd brushed against a rosebush filled with foraging bees. She still carried a deep fear of the creatures, and she ran straight for the nearest safe place she knew. Dashing out of the orchard and through a small copse, she headed for a rocky outcropping at the bottom of a dell.

Her eyes sought for the large, round rock she remembered from so many years ago. It was so exquisitely balanced that it could be rolled to one side within a narrow channel carved for the purpose untold years before. Dodging a bee, she shoved against the boulder and heaved, but the thing wouldn't move. Someone had wedged it shut with a smaller rock.

She felt the sharp pain of a bee sting on the back of her shoulder and cried out. Snatching the small rock away, Artemis fought off a growing panic and braced her shoulder against the boulder again.

It moved, revealing a dark cavity beyond.

Ducking inside, she let the boulder roll back into place. She stood, panting in the small space and rubbing at the painful lump already forming on her shoulder, thankful there had been only one sting. She looked about her.

Weak light streamed through the crevices in the rocks above, enough for her to see a little. Discovered by Orion as a boy, the forgotten escape tunnel was cleverly disguised. After swearing her to secrecy, he'd shown it to her. The passage had been a delicious secret to them, and they'd spent many hours playing there as children.

Hoping he still used the passage, she groped for the small lamp and light box he'd kept there long ago. Finding them quickly, she worked to light the lamp, offering a fervent prayer that it would work after all these years. It did.

The creamy yellow flame made the shadows leap and dance across the gray stone walls, but she had enough light to see an improvement had been made to the "door" of the tunnel. The rock, which had wedged it shut, could now be set in place from the inside or outside. A small hole through which the rock could pass had been laboriously drilled in the rock—a new addition from the time when they were children. She smiled. Apparently, Orion still used the passage from time to time.

Thank goodness. She intended to use the tunnel to escape *into* the house, and she wasn't certain which would be worse: picking her way past spiders, rats, and who knew what else might have lurked in an unused tunnel, or facing the bees. With relief, she set out, the lamp held high.

The Stonechase escape tunnel wound under the ground for a time and then began a slow spiral upward. Rough stone gave way to rough masonry and, finally, to the stone and wood of Stonechase Manor itself. Climbing the stairs, she took care to step lightly, unwilling to make any noise that might alert anyone to her presence behind the walls of Stonechase Manor. She didn't know if Orion had divulged the secret of the passage to anyone else. Perhaps he had kept its existence to himself. If so, she did not wish to break her long-ago promise to keep it secret, even a promise made as a child.

The passage had several openings. She put her ear to the listening horn at the first concealed door. Voices, many of them. With the inclement weather, a parlor had been set up as a card room. It sounded as though it were full. The sounds coming from the second horn sounded more like an afternoon soiree than a library.

She climbed higher. A panel that opened into a hallway was no good; the guests were strolling the halls restlessly, wandering from the gallery to the card room to their chambers.

When she did finally ascend to a deserted room, it was a guest's bedchamber. Though it was presently unoccupied, she was loathe to enter it. She stood quivering with indecision, unsure which would be worse: facing the bees or facing Orion, were she discovered in someone else's bedchamber uninvited. She shuddered and started up the passage once more.

At last the candle revealed the first sure safe point of exit, Orion's own bedchamber. If she were seen exiting that room, it would raise eyebrows, to be sure. She went on. Finally, she came to the garret exit, but the latch did not function. Upon closer inspection, she discovered the latch had been deliberately disabled from the inside. Of course. She should have anticipated Orion would protect his secret passage.

She could not open the door without making noise and risking discovery. And she'd be willing to wager every other door latch in the passage had been disabled, too. So Orion's chamber was her only option, unless she wanted to try her luck with the bees. She rubbed her stinging shoulder and sighed.

If she were patient and careful, she'd be able to exit Orion's chamber covertly. And if she were seen, she would simply say she was there to consider the redecoration. Besides, she would be alone. Orion would not be with her, and thus the transgression could not have lasting consequences.

She descended until she reached the part of the passage just outside his chamber.

She paused for a moment, looking about her at the makeshift tables and shelves he'd fashioned as a boy—his laboratory, he'd called it. A smile on her face, she held the candle higher, chasing away the shadows, and took a closer look, widening her eyes.

Stars and signs, the laboratory was still in use! Gone were the endless crocks pilfered from the gardens and kitchens and filled with everything from shiny pebbles to slimy tadpoles. Now the shelves in Orion's secret place were lined with neatly labeled jars of powders and liquids.

The crates of candles, makeshift tools, and broken odds and ends had given way to an impressive assortment of shiny crucibles, balances, thermometers, and microscopes alongside several small wooden boxes labeled in what looked to be Latin. Bugs, she'd wager. This was no longer just a little boy's fancy, but a grown man's passion.

Suddenly, the door opened. She gasped.

Light slashed across the floor, and Orion filled the doorway. "Artemis!"

"Orion! You scared me!"

*"I* scared *you?"* he said with a grin and pinched his nose. "I did not think you remembered this place! What are you doing in here?"

She laughed. "I am seeking a way out, truth to tell." She explained about the bees.

"Poor girl, you must have been frightened," he said. "You always were nervous around bees when we were children."

"Hmm! I see I am not the only one with a good memory."

"It is not difficult to keep such pleasant memories." He smiled warmly. "We had a lovely time tormenting each other back then."

She nodded and grinned. "Indeed."

"And yet"—he paused to move one of his glass vials a half inch in one direction—"we did spend at least part of our time in harmony."

"You trusted me back then."

He turned to her. "I still do."

"I cannot imagine why. Not after what I did last night."

"And I cannot imagine why you will even speak to me today, after my own behavior."

"You had reason to be angry."

"Not enough to shout and call you stupid."

"Agreed." She sighed. "See here, I really am trying. I promise to keep trying to fit in."

"I am afraid the *ton* won't easily forget last night."

"I am sorry."

"I know. Thank you." He shrugged. "Onward. You try not to read palms, and I will try not to be such an inconsiderate prig."

She laughed.

"Laughter," he said. "It feels like balm on an angry bee sting."

"What do you mean?"

"I have been out of sorts since I shouted at you last night. It wasn't just my irritation at having bent decorum so spectacularly. Nor your fortune-telling. Or even that asinine wager I allowed myself to be drawn into. All of those things added to my distemper, but the worst of it was the anger between us. I did not sleep well last night. And now, listening to you laugh, my heart is lighter."

He opened his mouth to say something more and then simply returned her smile instead.

She marveled at the change in him. "You seem to be a different person this morning." His carriage wasn't so proud, his eyes were warmer.

"I do not like being angry with you, Gypsy. I am glad we talked things through."

"No, it is more than that. Now you seem more like the Orion I used to know. Why? Is it this place?" She gestured around her.

He nodded. "This place . . . and you." He lit a pair of lamps. "This has always been the only place I can be myself. And you," he said with a shrug and a smile, "were always the only one besides my own mother who did not laugh at me or seem to think me odd."

"Odd? Of course you were odd. But odd does not mean unpleasant. Your mental gifts are wondrous indeed." She tucked a lock of her hair behind her ear. "Can you still . . ."

He threw her a cocksure look and raised one eyebrow. "Try me."

"Very well. Let me see now . . . six hundred seventy-one, and eight hundred ninety-three."

"One thousand five hundred sixty-four," he said without a second's hesitation.

Artemis rolled her eyes to the ceiling and closed one eye to do the mental calculation herself. "Show-off," she said after a few moments.

"You asked," he said with a smug smile.

She dipped her head with a smile of acknowledgment and then shook her head in wonder. "You could add and subtract numbers like that before I could count to one hundred. How do you do it so quickly?''

He shrugged. "I do not know. After you left—" He shook his head. "No, after you were driven away, I acquired the ability to multiply and divide just as rapidly.''

"Oh, my!" she marveled. "It is odd . . . in a very good way," she said. "I wish I could do it. I recall being quite fascinated with it when we were young. Stars and signs, I was forever pestering you to perform for me, wasn't I?" She laughed. "I was not very sorry then, but I am now, Orion."

"I am not. The truth is I was quite insufferably proud of my arithmetical abilities, and I was pathetically happy to have an appreciative audience for my peculiar talent.''

"*Talents.* Plural! You also had your music. Where is your harp?" she asked, looking about the room, trying to spot the ancient harp Orion had found in the tunnel.

According to the inscription on it, it had belonged to one Aelis de Chase, an ancestor of Orion's, no doubt. He had been born with a natural talent for the instrument, it seemed, almost as though his ancestor had left her own talent in the tunnel along with the harp, for Orion had been able to play simple songs on the thing well nigh instantly. He'd spent many hours amusing Artemis with his little songs.

"If your skill at arithmetic increased, then you must be a wonderful harpist by now."

He said nothing.

"You do still play, do you not?"

His smile faded. "No."

"Why not?"

He turned away, ostensibly to dust his microscope, but she could hear sadness in his voice as he said, "I did not play well."

"I do not believe you. You played beautifully, even as a little boy. Your ability with the harp was just like your ability with mathematics. You were born with them. Your skill with numbers did not go away, it increased, and I do not believe your skill at music simply left you, either."

He turned back to her, his jaw set, his eyes hard. "You are correct. It did not. But music is meant to be performed and witnessed by others. Mathematics is more . . . private."

"Meaning the skill did not disappear at all. You just concealed it."

"Yes."

"Why?" she asked.

"I grew tired of being considered odd."

"Shakespeare was odd . . . and Mozart . . . and Aristotle."

"Point taken, Gypsy. But I am not Mozart."

"And I," she said, "am not laughing at you." She put her hand to her heart. "Please . . . where is the harp?"

He held her gaze for a moment and then turned to extract a leather satchel from a high shelf. He handed it to her. The small harp was inside, wrapped in layers of rich, black velvet. He had taken good care of it. Its dark wood glowed with polish and its silver tuning pins shone. Artemis ran her hand across the strings experimentally. "It is in tune." Which meant he still played. She held the harp out to Orion. "Play it for me. Please?"

His eyes softened. "For you."

The harp came to life in his hands as he played a sweet song she remembered from long ago.

"That was my favorite!"

"I know," he said with a smile and kept playing.

Suddenly, he came to a different part of the song. "I do not remember that part," she said. "You must have learned it after I left."

His fingers stilled. "The song was yet unfinished when you left."

"You mean you composed that song yourself?"

He shrugged. "You seemed to like it."

A fresh sense of wonder and amazement swept her. Not only had he played the harp so skillfully at only eight years of age, but he had also composed so skillfully? "Stars and signs!"

"Surprised?"

"Yes!"

He grinned. "Think I am odd?"

"Yes!" She laughed. "Wonderfully odd."

"In that case, I shall finish my song." The harp sang as his fingers resumed lightly dancing over the strings. "The song has a name," he said with a studied casualness.

"What is it?" she whispered.

The melody issued forth as sweet as honey. The seconds ticked on. Orion appeared not to have heard her question. What had he called the song? He had composed it for her. Had he named it *Artemis's Song*, perhaps? Or maybe *The Girl Who Went Away . . . Come Back, Gypsy . . .* or maybe, just maybe, something like *The Rose I Loved*? He would tell her, she knew, else he would not have brought the matter up. Impatient, she forced herself to wait.

But the song ended at last, and still Orion did not volunteer the song's title.

"It was lovely," she said, "whatever its name."

"It is called"—he paused dramatically, and she held her breath—"as near as I can recall, the title I gave it was . . . *Good Riddance Silly Gypsy You Are Ugly Hope I Never See You Again Because You Smell Like a Stink Beetle.*"

"How romantic," she said dryly.

"A little forgiveness is in order, Gypsy. I was quite peeved with you at the time. I did not understand why you left and felt you had abandoned me. I can rename the song, if you wish."

"Oh . . . no," she said, laughing. "I quite like the title as it is."

He laughed along with her, and for the first time

since she had returned to Stonechase, he felt completely happy. In spite of all the trouble she had caused him, in spite of all the bad temper he had shown her, they were friends, and they would still be friends when they ended their sham betrothal, he was sure of it.

He was glad she had returned. It pained him to think how she and Anna might have ended up had Artemis not stopped at Stonechase. And if her safety and happiness meant he had to endure a little ridicule back in London, so be it.

Everything would be fine for her now. She would stay on as a part of his mama's household. His mama truly enjoyed her company, and she adored Anna. The three of them would bump along happily together, and, though he would no doubt suffer some loss of status, Orion would return to his old life in London—after he won that silly wager at Epiphany, of course.

Yes, everything was simple once more. Uncomplicated.

Artemis's laughter subsided at last, and she gestured toward his latest experiment. "What are you up to these days?"

"Studying feverfew."

"Flowers? I thought bugs were more the thing."

"They are, silly girl," he said without rancor. "Feverfew has known repellent qualities. I am conducting experiments to isolate and heighten the effect. It has great potential to increase crop production."

"It is also proof you have not fundamentally changed"— she stepped close to him and touched his heavily embroidered waistcoat with her fingertips—"despite the fashionable façade you try so desperately to maintain." To his complete surprise, she brought her other hand up to his waistcoat and, flattening her palms against his chest, she reached up and brought his head down, swarming into his arms and kissing him boldly.

Her scent, like flowers in the rain, swirled and blended in his mind with the feel of her lithe body and the softness of her lips, the warmth of her sweet breath, and Orion kissed her back with a passion that seemed to come out of nowhere.

For once he did not stop to analyze the situation. He simply let the moment pass as it would, a spell of warmth and emotion long denied welling from deep down. He did not attempt to stop it, ignore it, or even to hide it. He knew any attempt to hide the passion he felt would be futile anyway, for here was the person who knew him best.

When the kiss ended, he tucked her head under his chin. She snuggled close. "Why is it," he asked, "that the only person who truly understands me is someone as illogical as you?"

"Destiny does not have to be logical, Orion."

Destiny? He suddenly felt cold, and the room came back into focus. The spell between them was broken. He stepped away from her.

"We are not destined for each other, Artemis, for there is no such thing as destiny."

"Oh, but there is!"

"You will never convince me of that. Never in a thousand years. In spite of"—he hesitated—"in spite of the obvious passion there exists between us, we are wrong for each other. Complete opposites."

With a sly smile, Artemis flicked a bar magnet suspended from a string over his worktable and left without saying another word, the magnet spinning wildly behind her. Her message was clear: it was a law of nature that opposites attract.

He swore and quit his laboratory, knowing it would do him no good to attempt any research that day. The house party was coming to an end. After last night's announcement of Ophelia Robertson's wager ball, the guests had something delicious to look forward to and to prepare for, and a large contingent of them were in their rooms preparing for their journeys home. Orion decided to go downstairs and politely hasten their departures as much as possible. He was tired of the entire damnable charade, and the sooner the guests left, the sooner he could stop pretending.

Except that the pretending was just beginning, he grimly realized a few hours later, as he walked into the winter parlor and saw Artemis there, stitching quietly. The pace of the exodus had increased as he'd hoped, and for once she was alone. Her dark hair shone in the afternoon sunlight slanting through the window. She was dressed becomingly in a white gown with crimson trim, her face framed in dark curls. As she looked down at her work, her dark lashes dusted her white skin, and her delicate hands worked with precision and a calm he certainly did not feel.

His insides were once more in a tumble just from seeing her. He wanted to kiss her again, he realized. Hell, what he wanted was to carry her upstairs to his bed. But even as the thought occurred to him, he knew there was more to his feelings than raw desire. They truly were friends.

Thankfully, he still had just enough of a hold on his wits to know that desire, even paired with friendship, was not enough on which to base a successful marriage. A couple had to possess a measure of compatibility as well. They would be forever at odds, pitting destiny with free will, luck with coincidence, the signs with logical deduction. Their differences were just too great.

But so was his desire.

Inwardly, he groaned. Desire had the power to set reason to nought. What if she kissed him again? Would he be able to control his passion and thrust her away from him? What if he kissed her back? What if they were discovered and it was after they had broken their betrothal? She would be ruined if he did not marry her.

He would just have to avoid her at all costs, but— hell and blast!—avoiding her entirely would be impossible with her a part of his mother's household. Suddenly, an idea occurred to him. Perhaps he should give her exactly what she wanted . . .

Obviously sensing his presence, Artemis looked up from her embroidery. "Hello, Orion."

"Artemis." He nodded and sat opposite her. "It is time we settled the matter of the stakes of our wager."

Wariness filled her eyes. "Go on."

"If you win, I marry you—"

The wariness evaporated. "Oh, Orion! My darling!"

"—but if *I* win," he said, raising his voice, "you take twenty thousand pounds from me and disappear. You can live in Bristol, Exeter, York, or settle in the country—whatever you wish—but you will leave my mother's employ and never venture to London, Bath, or Brighton again."

"Done."

He frowned. "Just like that? You agree?"

"Of course, silly. Why would I not?" She stood up, clasped her hands together over her chest and spun around joyfully. "Oh, Orion, we shall be so happy together." She swept over to him and placed her hands over his. "You have made me very happy already."

Orion was worried. She was going to be broken-hearted when she lost their wager. Hell and blast, she would probably weep. He hated women's tears. They rent his soul. He would never learn how to handle them dispassionately. Never in a thousand years.

# CHAPTER
# FOURTEEN

With Christmas approaching, everyone at Stonechase was in high spirits. If they were not hanging kissing boughs or singing carols, they were preparing for the wedding—and trying to hide it from Orion. Yes, everyone was in high spirits—everyone but Orion himself.

Which is why, when he received word two days later that the prince had gone to Brighton for the holiday, he dressed with his usual care and ordered his things packed and the coach brought round and readied for the same journey. He waited in the library.

Inevitably, his mother caught wind of his plans and swooped down upon him, accompanied by Ophelia Robertson, who had stayed on at Stonechase Manor even after she had tucked their prediction envelopes into her enormous décolletage the day after their wager. The two of them, Mrs. Robertson and his mother, had hit it off. Yet, as much as he loved and admired them both, he was certain their continued friendship was going to be a thorn in his side.

"Orion," his mother wailed, "how *could* you? How

could you take Artemis and Anna away on their first Christmas home?"

"Artemis and Anna are staying here, Mama."

"Oho!" Mrs. Robertson crowed. "So that is how the land lies! I see."

"What," he drawled, "do you mean by that?"

"What Ophelia means," his mama said, "is that you had no idea Artemis was going with you. Did you?"

He scowled. "Of course I did," he lied.

"He did not." Artemis sailed through the door with Anna grinning on her hip. "He had planned to leave us behind."

"For shame," his mother intoned.

"Shocking," Mrs. Robertson said, grinning.

Orion sighed and pinched the bridge of his nose. "My dear ladies, my status within society is rather precarious just now, as you well know. Since the fashionable place to be is with the prince in Brighton, that is where I am going. And I would prefer to go alone," Orion added, trying to sound reasonable.

"You are betrothed," his mama said. "People will think it odd to see you apart from your fiancée."

"We will soon be parted for good, and people will think it natural."

"If you are going, I am going," Artemis said with a stubborn tilt to her chin.

"So am I," the countess said. "Coming, Ophelia?"

"Delicious! How can I refuse?" Mrs. Robertson asked, moving to stand shoulder to shoulder next to her allies.

They were bluffing, attempting to force him to stay.

"Suit yourselves," Orion said and made for the door. In the gleaming surface of his desk, he could see the three of them trade looks of alarm. He smiled. "I leave within the hour," he said, "with or without you." There was no way a countess, an old lady, a young lady, a nurse, a Gypsy, and a baby girl could all be ready to travel in an hour.

He was certain of it.

He was wrong.

They *were* ready to go. In fact, they were already waiting for him when he emerged from the house an hour later, the nurses and maids in their own coach with the baggage tied on top and his mama, Artemis, and Mrs. Robertson, with Anna on her lap, in the lead coach. He stared. This had to be Mrs. Robertson's doing. She must have known about the prince's plan to spend Christmas at Brighton all along. She had alerted his mama, for clearly they'd been ready.

Even now, the two older women wore smug expressions. He scowled and thought briefly of taking a seat with the servants, but discarded the idea. As tempting as it was to thwart their plan to push the two of them together, sitting with the nurses and abigails and baggage was deucedly unfashionable. He would not arrive in Brighton so.

He looked at Artemis, who, for her part, sat playing with Anna, a happy, innocent expression shaping her features. He had no doubt she *was* innocent. Because she believed it was their destiny to wed, she would have no reason to attempt to maneuver him.

He took a little comfort from that line of reasoning, for it led him to the conclusion that his mother and Mrs. Robertson didn't in truth believe in that destiny nonsense, for if they did, they'd have no reason to intervene. They would simply let life take its unalterable, inevitable course.

He smiled and climbed into the lead coach. "Lovely day for traveling, isn't it?"

"For now," Artemis said. "It is going to rain."

"Impossible. The atmospheric pressure is rising."

"You should listen to her," his mama said. "Her tea leaves said rain."

A mile or so from home, it did rain. Sort of. Anna promptly drooled on his boots, ruining their mirrorlike shine. The females, it seemed, were in league to annoy him as much as possible.

As they drove south for a time and then within an ace of due east along the coastal road, gulls screeched overhead, and the ever-present wind carried a refreshing salty tang. Orion loved the sea, but he rarely got to enjoy it. Alas, today was no exception.

He had reached a crossroads in his research on feverfew. He could pursue one line of reasoning or another, and he still was not certain which he should choose. It required some deep thought, and, though the ladies were occupied with needlework and left him blessedly alone to his thoughts, he still could not concentrate. They were using the stockings—the ones that had been flung from the coach—to fashion some doll clothes for Anna. They were attaching tiny silver bells to the doll clothes, and, as they worked, the bells' random jingling pierced his thoughts as neatly as a spider skewered a fly. He could not concentrate.

*"Can you not keep those blasted bells silent?"* he finally snapped.

All three ladies stared at him in shock. Anna's face crumpled and she began to cry, her eyes welling over with tears that seemed large enough to Orion to flood the interior of the coach. She was normally a happy little thing, and he hadn't seen her cry yet. He felt as though his heart were being ripped from his chest.

"Poor baby girl," Mrs. Robertson crooned. "The big, loud, cross man is not cross with you, dearling."

"Oh, Anna, of course not, sweet girl. I am sorry," Orion said. "Here now, would you like to come sit on my lap and play with my watch?" He took the shiny timepiece and its ornate fob from his pocket and dangled it enticingly. Immediately, Anna's face brightened, and she squirmed from the old lady's lap to his, where she proceeded to ignore the watch and promptly ruin his cravat, instead. He let her.

What was wrong with him? Shouting at ladies and scaring children?

As Anna untied and drooled on his cravat, he watched

Artemis interacting with his mama and Mrs. Robertson. Three peas in a pod they were, all the same. Spontaneous, unconventional, and outspoken. It had always been a challenge to his social status to be associated with his independent and unconventional mama, and now she had the flamboyant and outrageous Mrs. Robertson to encourage her wildness. Orion dreaded the result.

The thought of appearing with them in Brighton was enough to give him a megrim, but that wasn't the worst of his trouble. No. The fact that he'd once more be paired with Artemis after everyone had witnessed her display of Gypsy table manners, his disastrous display of temper, and their subsequent argument was outside of enough. Add to it Mrs. Robertson's blasted wager, which would be on the tips of everyone's tongue.

How had he made so many mistakes?

It was a mistake to have allowed himself to become betrothed to a Gypsy in the first place. Artemis *was* a Gypsy. She would always be a Gypsy.

He thought back to the way she had looked when she'd come to them at Stonechase: worn, dusty boots, a close-fitting embroidered chemise stretched over her ample bosom, a swirling black skirt, colorful scarves at her waist and shoulder. All Gypsy, as though she had just stepped from a caravan—which, of course, she had.

Today, she was dressed in a lovely lavender and white gown, her hair tamed with a matching ribbon and coaxed into a becoming halo of shiny dark curls. She spoke eloquently, moved with natural grace. On the outside, she was like any other well-born young lady— polite, soft-spoken, properly gowned—but she was still a Gypsy where it counted, on the inside. She would never fully rid herself of her Gypsy ways, and she would never be fully accepted by the *ton*, either.

Thank goodness their false betrothal was nearly at an end!

Looking up, Artemis caught his eye and smiled. Though he made an honest attempt to return the smile, he knew he had failed from the questioning, slightly troubled look she gave him. Pretending not to have noticed her expression, he turned his attention to the scenery.

They had just passed through a small seaside village and were rolling through an area of farmland that marched right down to the sea. On one side, the fields were sown with winter crops, while on the other the road gave way to a low, sandy cliff. Approaching a small stream, the road dived over a low, arching stone bridge. From the peak of the bridge, Orion could glimpse the ocean below and ahead of them. The water was dark gray with the wind's turbulence.

Suddenly, the driver of the second coach gave a shout and all of the equipages lurched to a stop. A rope securing the baggage had jolted loose. As they watched, a small brown trunk slid off the back of the second coach and down over the steep embankment. It slid over the deep grass before jouncing down over some rocks and splashing into the sea.

A shrill screech rent the air, and Artemis scrambled out of the lead coach. "Oh! Stars and signs!" she cried, looking over the edge of the bridge into the water below. And then, to everyone's astonishment, Artemis jumped into the sea.

For a moment, no one moved or made a sound. The next instant, the air was full of shouts of alarm. Skirts flew and hats jarred loose as everyone came off and out of the coaches and cart to stand staring in dismay over the low wall of the bridge and down into the water.

Orion's mind focused and instantly clicked into action. He vaulted over the low wall and onto a rock protruding from the cliff side, where he could get a better view. Far below, the little stream widened at its mouth, forming a small protected cove just beyond the bridge.

Artemis struggled in the gray water of the relatively calm cove. She was clearly attempting to save the bobbing trunk, which was being carried by a swift current parallel to the shore. She was obviously a good swimmer, but, hampered as she was by her sodden clothes, she wasn't making any headway. She was, however, staying afloat well enough, and it was easy to see that, within moments, the current would carry both her and the trunk onto the small beach behind the lip of the cove.

In a fraction of a second, Orion had assessed the tide, the current, the probable depth, and temperature of the water, and Artemis's ability to swim, coming to the conclusion that she was not in any real danger. He could wait right where he was and she would be fine. She'd be carried to the little beach, whether she wanted to go there or not, and then the footmen would help her back up the steep embankment or walk her far enough upstream to make a climb unnecessary. She was in no danger.

And yet, the next moment, a surprised Orion suddenly found himself flying through the air. He had jumped from his nice, warm, dry rock—and he was royally annoyed with himself for having done so.

Though the frigid water made him gasp, he cut through the waves without pause and, gaining Artemis's side, took hold of the back of her gown's neckline. "Try to float on your back," he ordered. "I will pull you to shore."

But the stubborn chit did not meekly roll onto her back. She fought him!

"Are you trying to drown us both?" he cried.

"The trunk!" she shouted. "Save the trunk first!"

Orion ignored her, of course, and they struggled against each other all the way to the small slice of pebbly beach at the mouth of the cove. She struggled to her feet, her eyes fixed on the trunk, and marched back toward the water. Orion clamped his hand on her arm and hauled her back around. "What is so important about that trunk? What is in it? A few gowns? A bonnet or two? Can you be so shallow?"

"You do not understand, Orion," she cried, her teeth chattering. "You *must* save that trunk!"

At that moment, it started to rain.

"Dear me, are you both in one piece?" Mrs. Robertson called.

"We both appear to be unhurt!" Orion called back. He raked his fingers through his wet hair, pulling out a clump of seaweed in the process. He looked at the trunk, which was making much slower progress toward the beach than they had, and then he looked at Artemis. Her gown, wet and caked with sand, clung to her skin. A glob of seaweed and knotted hair hung over her face. "You are shivering."

His mother called down to him, "Orion, bring her here at once! She will catch her death!"

He looked up and called back, "Whereas *I* am in no danger, Mama?"

"Oh, Orion!" she said. "Of course I want you to live—"

"That is better."

"—elsewise . . ." she began, laughing, "elsewise, poor Artemis could never become the new countess!"

Orion rolled his eyes. "I am going to hug you for that, Mama, just as soon as I climb back up the hill."

"You are wet and cold!" she protested.

"Exactly," Orion called. "Come, Gypsy," he held out his hand. "I will help you climb the hill."

Artemis looked stricken and glanced back over her shoulder at the trunk. He could not be certain, for she was already wet, but he thought he saw a tear grow in the corner of her eye.

"Oh, all right . . . blast! Why not? I am already wet." He trudged back into the cold, swirling sea and retrieved the trunk. It was not very seaworthy and had partially filled with water. Grasping one of the tarnished brass handles, he tugged. It was easy work until he reached the pebbly shore, but then it was deucedly heavy, and it took a great effort to bring it up onto the sand. His anger grew with each savage pull he gave it.

"Oh!" Artemis wailed. "It is filled with water! It will be ruined!"

Bent at the waist, his hands braced on his knees, he panted and eyed the trunk, suddenly realizing the thing looked familiar. It ought to, by Jove. It was his!

Artemis was crying in earnest now, and he was suddenly blazingly angry.

"What," he thundered, "could be so important in that trunk—*my* trunk!—that you would risk drowning to save it?!"

He yanked open the trunk and stilled in shock, for there in the trunk was his microscope, in several jagged and bent pieces. Wooden boxes of insects had broken, liberating their prisoners, and what must have been all of his powdered feverfew jars had broken, giving the seawater a milky appearance. His special, bright-burning candles floated in the opaque water.

He fell to his knees beside the trunk. *Ruined. All ruined. Four years of research.*

A strangled sound escaped Artemis beside him, and he looked up. Her eyes were full of misery.

"I wanted to surprise you," she said, her voice half whisper, half sob. "I knew you were fleeing Stonechase because of me, and I knew you would be unhappy to leave your laboratory behind." Her words came out in a torrent. "So . . . so I packed it all up so you could take it with you, and now . . . now everything is ruined," she wailed, "and I should never have touched your things and—oh, Orion!—I am so sorry!"

She covered her face.

So there they were. His experiment lay in ruins. They were both soaked with seawater and caked with sand. His best Hessians were historical objects. Artemis was sobbing into her hands with seaweed hanging ridiculously from her ear, and he knew damned well he looked no better. They were only a few miles away from Brighton on the busy coastal road, and they were starting to draw a crowd in spite of the rain that, coming down harder now, had driven the other members of their party back into the coaches. Glancing up, Orion scanned the bridge. A dozen faces stared back down at him: four or five servants from Stonechase and a few curious travelers newly arrived on the scene.

His heart sank.

*Whitemount.*

Catching Orion's eye, the viscount doffed his hat, a malicious, leering smile spreading across his face. And then he simply turned and rode on, on toward Brighton, where he would no doubt relate the scene he'd witnessed over and over in excruciatingly delicious detail.

Orion blinked. His situation had never been worse.

He should have been comfortless and miserable, lost and defeated. And yet, in that moment, as Artemis continued to bawl out an inconsolable apology, clearly crushed that she was responsible for destroying his microscope and drowning his "bugs," as she called them, something amazing happened. Something he could never have foreseen.

Something irrational. Unreasonable. Completely illogical.

He realized he loved her.

Who else but Artemis would have done such a madcap thing as jumping into the sea to save his microscope and insects? Who else knew about them in the first place? And even if the whole world had known about them, who else would have packed the blasted things?

No one.

Artemis Rose was the only person on earth who truly understood him or who ever truly would. In a flash of realization, he knew she had always understood. His heart swelled with gratitude, esteem, and delighted affection. He loved her, by Jove, he loved her! More than Marianna Grantham. More than his bugs, even. He loved the silly Gypsy more than anything.

Grasping her hand, he pulled her into his arms and hugged her to him.

"Orion?" she cried.

*Marry me.*

The words flashed through his mind a split second before they came to his lips. He opened his mouth to utter them . . .

And then, before he could make any wild declarations, the logical part of his mind surfaced once again.

It was true: Artemis did understand him, but that understanding went both ways. He knew her well enough to know he could never make her happy.

The *ton* would never fully accept her, and since he was a part of the *ton*, neither would he. He could never accept her in all of her spontaneous glory. Her behavior would always embarrass him, and she would have to endure a life knowing her husband disapproved of her. Even if he tried to hide it, she knew him well enough to see right through such a pretense. Marrying her just wouldn't be fair.

"Thank you, Artemis." He smiled, feeling as though he might weep himself. "I know you tried to please me. The microscope can be replaced, and the . . . the bugs are easily found in any corn patch. No harm done," he lied.

"Certain?"

"I am certain," he said, though what he was actually certain of was that his heart would never mend.

"Is none of it salvageable?" Artemis asked.

"I do not know. Let us have a better look, shall we?" Tipping the trunk, he drained the water onto the pebbly sand.

Artemis groaned. "Nothing appears to have escaped destruction. Even the lining of your trunk is—" She stopped suddenly and, reaching into the trunk, pulled a square of sodden yellow paper from where it had been wedged behind the trunk's sagging green satin lining.

"What is that?" Orion asked.

"An envelope," she said, peering closely at the envelope with knitted brows, "and it appears to have my handwriting on it, though I do not remember having—" She stilled, her eyes growing round and wide. She blinked. And then, suddenly, her face clouded over with fury. "Orion . . . how could you?"

"What?"

"How could you steal my wish boat?"

"Your what?"

"My wish boat! This," she said, waving the envelope, "was in my boat. You took it, you . . . you pirate!"

"What boat?"

"You have forgotten, you scoundrel. It meant nothing to you, so you stole it and promptly forgot it. That snow was cold, Orion."

She wasn't making sense. "What snow, Gypsy?"

"I lay in the snow to make ten snow angels. Ten! I was cold. There you were, planning to steal the boat anyway, and yet you made me freeze my backside making an army of snow angels to guide the boat. And what about my wish? You stole that from me, too, you beast."

The beast suddenly remembered what she was talking about. "Oh! Your boat," he said. "If you want to call it that. As I remember, it was little more than a ball of sticks and twine."

"If you thought so little of it, why did you steal it?"

"I did not."

"Then how do you explain this?" She waved the envelope in the air some more.

"Your flimsy boat became hopelessly stuck ten yards from where you launched it. I took it to save you from the realization that your silly wish would never come true. The envelope must have fallen into my trunk somehow."

He expected her face to fold into that most feminine expression of warmth and sentiment, the one where ladies' eyes grew warm, their brows wrinkled, and their mouths smiled while still managing to form the most delicate *O*. Warmth and sentiment, however, weren't what Artemis wished to express. More like horror and outrage.

"How could you interfere like that?" she demanded. "The boat might have broken free."

"Yes, and it might have sunk to the bottom and rotted. See here, the thing could barely float. Its chances of making it to the sea were minuscule."

"But not zero."

"No," Orion conceded, "not zero."

"Well then, you should have left it right where it was. Surely, Lord Logic, you can comprehend that plucking it from the brook and absconding with it left it absolutely no chance of—" She stopped, her words forgotten.

He watched as her eyes became unfocused. She seemed to be frozen in place. She was no longer shivering, and he could have sworn she wasn't even breathing. Then, she blinked once . . . twice. Her eyes softened, and a slow contented smile stole across her face.

"Of course," she murmured.

Instantly wary, Orion narrowed his eyes at her. "What are you so amused about?"

Suddenly, a shaft of sunlight broke through the clouds and shone down upon them. She raised her face and inhaled deeply, as though she were breathing in sunshine, and then she let go of a beautiful, wide smile.

"You are forgiven, Lord Logic, for my wish envelope *did* make it to the sea, after all." She waved the envelope toward the sodden trunk. "It simply did not arrive the way I had planned. My wish *will* come true," she said, "and you, Orion, are the one who made that possible. Oh, look! A sun shower!" She tilted her head back. Rain dropped through the sunshine and splashed onto her face, and she laughed as though she hadn't a care in the world.

"What did you wish for?" he asked sourly.

She closed her eyes and shook her head. "Uh-uh.

Have I taught you nothing? I cannot tell the wish. It has not yet come true."

"Oh," Orion drawled. "How silly of me."

With a sly smile, Artemis straightened and stuffed the envelope up her wet sleeve. "Not to worry. I promise to the reveal its contents later—after the wish has come true."

"Capital," he said as the blasted rain pattered down. "I shall hold my breath."

# CHAPTER FIFTEEN

As a man at the van of society, Orion's surprise betrothal to Artemis had created quite a stir. They were both notable figures—Orion, the pink of the *ton*, and Artemis, at once the granddaughter of an earl and a Gypsy. Within an hour of arriving at their rented house in Brighton, the entire party had received an invitation to stay at the Pavilion as guests of the prince.

"Do not be nervous, my gel," Mrs. Robertson said, as she and Lady Lindenshire accompanied Artemis through the pavilion's cavernous halls.

"You look lovely," the countess assured her.

It was evening. Music welled up faintly from downstairs. In spite of Mr. Nash's extensive renovations then under way, the prince's Marine Pavilion had a full complement of guests. Christmas had come and gone, and everyone had had a merry time—except for Orion, Artemis thought on a sigh.

Her fiancé had been pensive or sullen the entire time, and she was certain he had been avoiding her. Unfortunately, it was too much to hope he would continue the pattern and avoid her this evening! No, Artemis was certain that, as soon as he caught sight of her, he would bluster to her side and deliver a blistering set down.

"No one can fail to see the humor of your costume," Mrs. Robertson said.

Artemis gave a wry smile. "No one?"

"My son's sense of humor *is* rather impaired at times, Ophelia," Lady Lindenshire said.

Mrs. Robertson returned her smile. "I may have overstated," she conceded, "but Artemis will be a sensation, I vow, and your stubborn son shall be pleased in spite of himself."

It was two days before the new year, and the prince, on a whim, had announced a masquerade only that morning. A masquerade costume, it turned out, was the only thing Lady Lindenshire had forgotten to order from Madame Aneault. So, in a pinch, Artemis had made a bold decision to dress as a Gypsy. Every stitch of her clothing had been packed for Brighton, including her old clothes, which she had saved because her mother had made them.

To the old close-fitting red-embroidered chemise and black skirt, she had added things borrowed for the occasion from Mrs. Robertson: bright, fringed scarlet and spangled orange shawls, gaudy bracelets, a pair of large earrings, and a fan of vibrant green silk. Lady Lindenshire had suggested the addition of the dozen silver bells from the stockings and doll gown and had provided a necklace, a single large, fine ruby hanging on a heavy gold chain.

The costume was perfect.

With her black, wavy hair loose, the spangled shawls tied about her waist, and the bells and jewelry jingling as she walked, she looked—and sounded—very like a Gypsy at a festival.

"I *am* nervous, but I am more comfortable than I was last evening. Dressing as you tonnish Outsiders do is most disagreeable!"

The older women laughed.

The evening before, at supper, she had worn an expensive, exquisite creation of aqua and ultramarine silk with trim the colors of sunrise—delicate pinks and oranges. Her hair had been piled atop her head, with pearls glowing at her wrist, neck, and ears. She had been dressed as any young lady might have been, right down to her gloves, slippers, and stays, which itched; ostrich feather hair adornments, which swayed precariously and tickled the back of her neck; reticule, ridiculously useless because it was empty; and a fan, ridiculously useless because it was December. She had looked like any other young lady seated at the prince's enormous table, but she had not felt the same. She felt . . . different, and she supposed she always would, for she *was* different, and everyone knew it.

Everyone.

People she had never met had been approaching her since she arrived. They'd all heard of her wager with Orion, and, invariably, they wanted to ask the number she'd guessed. A few of the queries were genuine and good-natured, but most were slyly patronizing. She tried not to be annoyed with them. Most Outsiders, she supposed, had incomplete educations. Most regarded the signs as some mystical nonsense, which wasn't their fault. They just hadn't been exposed to the truth. Not yet. But tonight they would be.

At masquerades, Mrs. Robertson had explained, the guests were supposed to act the parts for which they dressed, which meant tonight Artemis would be expected to behave as a Gypsy! She smiled.

As the three ladies rounded the corner and entered the grand ballroom, a wave of murmurs followed them, echoing to the top of the cavernous bowed ceiling. Lady Lindenshire in her shepherdess costume and Mrs. Robertson as the Queen of the Nile pressed close.

"Easy, my gel . . . steady. They are just taking your measure."

"Where is Orion?" Artemis whispered. "Can you see him?"

"No," Lady Lindenshire said with a chuckle, "but I would wager my entire fortune that, wherever he is, *he* can see *us.*"

"You would lose that wager, my dear Belle," Mrs. Robertson said, "for I am certain your son cannot see *us* at all." She laughed.

"Quite right." The countess chuckled. "The only person in his universe at this moment is Artemis."

"You are not helping," Artemis said.

Both ladies laughed and, as though by some unspoken signal, veered away from her at the same moment, leaving Artemis conspicuously alone. She was not alone for long, however, for immediately, the masked *ton* converged.

Orion pretended not to see Artemis. Standing next to a tall window, he turned his back to her just as his mama and Mrs. Robertson left her standing alone. He could still see her in the reflection of the glass. He just wasn't about to acknowledge her. He didn't dare. He didn't think he could keep from shouting at her.

Their time together was coming to an end. Soon, he would win the wager and she would cease to be a part of his life once more. He did not wish to spend one second more of the time they had left in discord, but ... but dressing as a Gypsy, indeed! It was outrageous ... it was shocking ... it was—

It was probably Mrs. Robertson's doing.

Or his mother's.

Or both.

In spite of himself, he turned and eyed the orange spangled scarf that clung to Artemis's hips and then the familiar ruby necklace. Yes, she had definitely had their help, blast them.

"She is a lovely creature," a feminine voice murmured at his elbow.

It was Marianna Sinclair, and he realized that, for the first time since he'd met her, his heart wasn't doing curious little flip-flops at the sound of her voice.

He bowed. "Lady Trowbridge."

"*Lady Trowbridge?* Oh, please, do not be so formal, my dear Orion. I might begin to think you are still upset."

"No." He shook his head. "No, I am not. You are happier with Trowbridge than you would have been with me."

She nodded. "I made the right choice"—she lightly touched his sleeve—"for both of us, you and me. Our hearts were already taken, mine by my own pirate"—she nodded toward her husband, who was also dressed as a pirate, though a rather more wild-looking version than Orion's—"and yours by your Gypsy."

He shook his head. "No, no . . . you must not think I asked for your hand while I was in love with another. Artemis and I have only just become acquainted."

"You forget to whom you are talking, Orion—or should I call you Lord Logic?" Marianna said with a smile. "I am just as logical as you—"

"You are a remarkably intelligent woman."

"—and I also know Ophelia Robertson quite well," she finished.

Orion rolled his eyes. "How much did she tell you?"

"Not much. She did not mean to divulge anything important, to be sure, but she said enough for me to make certain deductions."

"Oh?"

"Indeed. And that which logic has not provided, the look in your eyes as you watch Miss Rose has." She followed Orion's gaze, which had found Artemis once more. "You do love her. And you have since you were children—though I am certain you doubt it even now."

"You think you know me so well?"

She gave him a piercing look. "I know one part of you, and it is not the part standing here. This Orion is too concerned with what others think of him. The Orion I met—the Orion I might have agreed to wed and grown to love, had I not already fallen in love with Truesdale—that Orion was more interested in natural science than in the comings and goings of the *ton*. But *this* Orion does not notice insects. Even if he did, he would not be able to see them properly because he does not wear his spectacles. Perhaps," she said with a kind, sad sort of smile, "you would see everything more clearly if you put them on—even if your eyes were closed."

The waltz ended, and her husband came to claim her for the next set. She smiled, brushed Orion's arm with her fingertips, and was gone.

Orion stared down at his quizzing glass for a moment. The blasted thing was fashionable and quite useful for cutting a fine dash, but it was bloody useless for helping him to see. On their own, his eyes could see things perfectly well from a distance, but everything within an arm's length was blurry, and Marianna was aware of that. But Orion knew she wasn't speaking of his eyesight at all.

She was speaking of his *in*sight.

Orion frowned and looked for Artemis, finding her in the center of a knot of people. Crossing the room ostensibly to procure a glass of lemonade, Orion drifted behind a potted rose arbor that had been forced into riotous bloom. He was near enough to hear what was being said at the center of the knot. And what he heard, he did not like.

A voice. The Viscount Whitemount's.

Orion peeked covertly through the arbor and spied Whitemount, who had come dressed as a pasha, complete with bejeweled turban and shoes that curled up at the toes.

"I commend you, my dear," he said loudly. He was talking to Artemis, but his tone was designed to carry.

"You have shown much improvement since the night I escorted you to the ball. You have learned the steps beautifully in so short a time. No more tripping, I see."

"Tripping?" someone asked.

"Oh my, yes!" Whitemount said. "Miss Rose stumbled as she danced that night, and she suffered a most grievous fall. I had to escort her home immediately. It was very severe. She thought she might have broken her ankle—or so she told me on way to Lindenshire's house. I had to examine it to ascertain if there were any breaks."

A speculative murmur rose from the crowd, and out of nowhere Mrs. Robertson and Orion's mother glided silently over to his side under the arbor, both wearing expressions of alarm. "But, of course," Whitemount continued, "my coach was closed and dark, and I could see precious little. The ankle *felt* fine, however," he said. "And the leg."

Orion flinched as anger seized him.

"Steady, my boy," Mrs. Robertson whispered. "Your gallantry would do nothing. He has said naught but the truth, after all. If you challenge him, it will go worse for you both."

His mama lay a hand upon his arm. "Artemis is clever," she whispered. "I wager she will take care of Whitemount by herself. Stay your hand. It is best to pretend you do not hear."

Orion flicked a glance at Whitemount and then nodded, forcing himself, with great effort, to inaction.

Artemis snapped her green fan closed. "I did not need your . . . *assistance,* my lord."

Whitemount sighed dramatically. "Oh, yes. You are fully recovered, I see, my dear. No lasting damage. And may I say you look in fine form this evening—though you must be terribly unhappy that your costume was ruined."

Artemis looked confused. "My costume?"

"Do not be modest, my dear! We all know your costume was lost when your baggage tumbled into the sea."

As Orion had known he would, Whitemount had told the tale over and over.

"No," Artemis said, shaking her head. "You are mistaken."

"Oh?" Whitemount said dramatically, not trying very hard to conceal his grin. "I thought that was why you jumped into the sea that day—to save your costume. Surely you would not risk your life just to save a trunk full of insects. Oh . . . forgive me, my dear. They were *your fiancé's* insects, were they not? I forgot. Your fiancé's insects are very important to him. Of *course* you would risk life and limb to save them."

"Orion's experiments are important," she said, anger humming in her voice.

"Oh, my dear, I do not doubt it, and I, for one, am glad you saved them. Still, I wish for your sake there had been a costume crammed into the trunk along with the bugs and potions. Poor dear. What you have on really isn't much of a costume, is it? Not much of a stretch for people to believe you really still are a Gypsy."

"Perhaps," she agreed with apparent chagrin.

Orion was not fooled. The sudden, dangerous glint in her eye was sharp as a rapier, and she had the wit to go with it. He knew instinctively that she was going on the attack. If he hadn't wanted to break the blackguard in half, he might almost have felt sorry for him.

"*However,*" she said looking Whitemount up and down, "I daresay it is much less of a stretch for people to believe I am a Gypsy than it is for them to believe *you* are a harem master, my lord."

The crowd that had been gathering less and less discreetly as Whitemount had prepared and loosed his sly siege now tittered and chuckled.

"Touché, my dear," Orion murmured.

"See?" his mother whispered. "She needs no rescuing."

But Whitemount didn't know when to quit. His eyes widened dramatically. "Oh, my . . . is that not the skirt you were wearing when we met? When you received me in the Earl of Lindenshire's parlor? It is such a charming garment. So very . . . charming." Pinching some snuff from his green enameled, parrot-shaped box, he smiled, and then, with a flourish, he brought the pinch to his nose and executed a healthy sniff—knocking his wig quite seriously askew.

Every pair of eyes widened. Several ladies' fans snapped open and rose simultaneously. Four or five gentlemen were taken with sudden fits of coughing. It was almost painfully obvious that Whitemount knew they were trying to hide their mirth about *something*, though he did not know what. A panicked look shaped his features for a moment, but *still* he did not know enough to retreat.

"Will you not make us some amusing predictions, my dear?" he asked. "Perhaps you have a crystal ball hidden beneath your *charming* skirt?"

A brilliant smile blossomed upon Artemis's glowing face. "I am afraid, my lord, I have left my crystal ball outside in the wagon—but perhaps *you* have something round and shiny I might gaze into."

The assembled guests folded into gales of laughter, no longer even attempting to hide it.

The prince emerged from the melée of merriment and half laughed, half spoke: "*I* will make a prediction, Whitemount—we shall soon be seeing more of you than we wish!"

The crowd howled with laughter, and Whitemount scowled, affronted. "Well!" he said, "if that is the way you feel about me, Your Royal Highness, then perhaps I should leave." He boldly held the prince's gaze.

The crowd stilled. It was clear Whitemount thought the prince would back down. He had been at first oars with the prince, and indeed with of all of Society, for several years. And yet the crowd sensed, as Orion did, a change on the wind.

The prince returned Whitemount's stare for a moment. His eyes flicked down at Artemis and then swept the crowd before returning to Whitemount once more. "This lady is welcome here, whether she becomes the Countess of Lindenshire or not. And you, Whitemount," he said, "are correct. As always."

Making a motion to the orchestra, the prince bowed to Artemis. "May I have the pleasure of this dance?"

Orion's mother sighed happily, Mrs. Robertson beamed, and both patted his hands as they moved off.

Artemis and the prince waltzed on, as George DeMoray, the Viscount Whitemount, faded from the room—and from society—like a fog at midday.

"*Unpleasant* man," Orion heard the old Countess Rangnor complain loudly to Sir Thomas Bartling. "Never could stomach the wretch."

"Not to worry," Sir Thomas said. "I doubt we shall see much of the Viscount Whitemount in Town from now on."

"Not where the prince is, at any rate." The countess nodded to where the regent was dancing opposite Artemis. "He seems to have taken a shine to Lindenshire's lady. Clever gel."

"*Pleasant* little thing," Sir Thomas agreed. "Always smiling. Reminds me of my own dear lady wife, rest her merry soul."

The dance ended, and the prince led Artemis from the floor. They sat together, ignored the refreshments that appeared instantly at their elbows, and Artemis bowed her head. What was she doing? Orion craned his neck to get a better view, and then almost groaned.

She was reading the prince's palm.

# CHAPTER SIXTEEN

He turned his back as old Countess Rangnor and Sir Thomas Bartling hurried toward the knot of people that formed around Orion's betrothed and the prince. They all wanted their futures told. He ignored the merry laughter that erupted from the cluster and the occasional startled cries of "How did she know that?" He even managed to remain impassive when Lady Devonshire called for trays of tea to be brought in "with plenty of leaf."

But when Mrs. Robertson and his mother headed toward the commotion, Orion could bear it no longer. Fortunately, he was faster.

Orion was also taller, and the plumed black pirate hat he wore made him look even more imposing—or perhaps it was his grim expression. The crowd recognized him and parted easily. Reaching the center of the cluster, he swept the hat from his head and executed a low bow. "My lords and ladies, I beg your pardon, but this pirate cannot resist stealing such a lovely treasure for himself." A waltz was playing, and, taking Artemis's small hand, he tugged her onto the dance floor and whirled her away to the far side of the room.

"Uh-oh," she said. "You are scowling."

"Pirates always scowl," he said, knowing they were closely observed, that every word would be noted.

"Not when they are dancing with Gypsies."

"*Especially* when they are dancing with Gypsies," he said. "Especially when they hate to dance," he added almost inaudibly.

"You really dislike dancing, then?" she asked.

"Yes."

"Then why dance at all?"

"Because is it fashionable to do so, Gypsy."

"Do you always do what is fashionable, my lord pirate?"

"I have betrothed myself to you, have I not? Gypsies are not very fashionable."

"I beg to differ," said a voice at his back. "Give way, Sir Pirate. I am stealing her back from you. You will have an entire lifetime with your fashionable Gypsy. You must allow me a second dance. And she waltzes so gracefully."

Orion bowed. "Your Highness." He was forced to step aside and allow the Prince Regent to sweep Artemis away, her bells jingling off into the din of the ballroom.

The prince did finish the waltz with Artemis, but then he promptly escorted her to a corner, where he pressed a teacup into her hands. An empty teacup, Orion did not doubt, one with "plenty of leaf" at the bottom. A line of guests formed behind the prince, a line of people holding teacups or looking at their own palms.

"I yield," Orion muttered. "I give up." He quit the room and made for the card room, where he proceeded to lose badly. But even there, he could not escape her. She was all anyone could talk about, it seemed, and word of her activity reached him whether he wished it to or not.

She was apparently making outrageous predictions for the new year, each one more shocking than the last:

The prince would move to America and live with the Indians.

The Countess of Rangnor would become an actress.

Sir Thomas Bartling would marry a woman twice his considerable age.

As the night wore on, Orion heard of six men who had danced with Artemis twice, and Prinny had proclaimed her an Original. People wandering into the card room singled Orion out to congratulate him over and over for his social prowess in snatching her up before any other gentleman could. She was a complete success, they said.

And yet Orion knew it would not last.

He was not fooled. Position in society was fluid, and the *ton* was terribly capricious. She was a success tonight, yes, but next week she could be an outcast, just like Whitemount. She was a Gypsy. She would always be a Gypsy. She would never try to hide what she was.

Unlike himself.

The thought was unwelcome.

What was wrong with attempting to shield himself from others' ignorance and disdain? He'd always been laughed at and made fun of for his interest in insects and his intellectual gifts. People didn't see them as gifts, like Artemis did, but as peculiarities. He'd always been on the outside of every group. What was wrong with having found a way to be inside the circle? Inside, hell! He was at the very center of the *ton*. What was wrong with that?

Nothing.

And—by Jove!—he would remain inside the circle by his wits, Gypsy fiancée or no.

Squaring his shoulders, he put a large stack of coin into the center of the card table and excused himself from the game he was playing. It was time to take charge of the mull. His reputation had taken a serious blow, and basking in the seclusion of the card room would not repair it. It was time to be seen. It was time to take charge of his future once more.

He found Artemis immediately. She wasn't difficult to spot. He simply looked for the largest cluster of people, knowing she would be found at its center. "Gypsy rubbish," he muttered. He invaded her circle, piercing the center as neatly as an arrow pierces the water.

"I wish to dance, my dear."

He wore a smile, and yet something in his manner or voice produced a wary look in her eyes. No one else seemed to notice. Smart girl. She held out her hand and, taking it, he led her onto the dance floor.

"I thought you hated to dance," she whispered.

"I love dancing."

Her eyes showed confusion, and she regarded him with a curious tilt of her head for a moment before one eyebrow rose, and she said, "Ah. You are back to lying once more."

He did not deny it. If that is what she chose to call his tonnish façade, that was her own business.

They danced. Waltzing seemed to be in the prince's favor this evening, and Orion whirled her around the room until she was breathless. People watched and murmured their appreciation as they passed. They were the most fascinating couple of the *ton*—at least for the moment. But Orion knew the *ton's* fascination with Artemis would pass.

She did not understand, did not see it coming, and she would be devastated.

If she were still a part of society. If she remained with his mother at Stonechase. Or married Orion.

But that, of course, could not happen. According to the terms of their wager, after Mrs. Robertson's ball, she would disappear from London society, and Orion would remain behind, still inside the circle. Still at the center.

He would miss her, but there was no other solution.

They could not marry without being forever at odds as he strove for the center of the circle and she hung, disapproved and disparaged, even by him, on the periphery.

Neither could they exist unmarried and still near each other. They would end up in each other's arms. He would kiss her—or worse—and they would end up married anyway. Married and miserable.

But even as the thought occurred to him, he looked into her dark, smiling eyes and knew there would be no escape from misery for him. It gave him some comfort to think Artemis would still have a full life. Her loveliness and her spontaneous, happy disposition, coupled with the fortune he would settle upon her as part of the terms of their wager, would surely leave her with no lack of suitors in Exeter or Bristol. She would be happy before long, and Orion would become a distant, pleasant memory.

"Orion?" she said, concern in her voice. "You look troubled. What is the m—" Her words were silenced by the ringing crash of an enormous gong that hung at the far end of the ballroom. Instantly, every conversation stopped, the orchestra silenced, and all feet stilled. As the reverberation of the gong faded, clocks could be heard striking the midnight hour all over the palace.

The prince smiled from atop a small dais near the gong and cleared his throat. "I have an announcement," he said. "Some interesting information to impart." He allowed the room to swell with murmured excitement before he went on. "It is now past midnight, and therefore it is the eve of the New Year—a date relevant to a certain wager well known to some."

It was an exaggeration, affected for dramatic effect. Everyone knew very well there wasn't a soul unaware of Orion and Artemis's very public wager.

The prince smiled. "I happen to know the exact number of betrothals that have occurred. Would you like to know the number?" he asked his guests. The company applauded enthusiastically, but Mrs. Robertson stepped forward, blustering.

"No!" she called out. "Prinny, you wouldn't!"

The prince laughed. "I would, my dear Mrs. Robertson. I would indeed. It is not often I best you." He bowed and gave the old woman a wink. "You shall just have to think of something else to entertain us at your ball."

"You bounder," Mrs. Robertson muttered, but not without affection.

The prince smiled and turned to Orion and Artemis. "And you, Lindenshire and Miss Rose? Do you wish to know the number?"

Orion nodded. "By all means—though I daresay I will be unsurprised." Scattered laughter erupted among the crowd.

"And you, Miss Rose?"

Artemis nodded, her expression uncharacteristically grim.

"Sixteen," the prince intoned.

"One off," Orion said. "I guessed seventeen." He turned to Artemis. Her expression fell. She bowed her head.

"You won, I think, Lindenshire," the prince said.

But suddenly Orion did not feel exultant.

"Pray tell," the prince said with his usual jovial charm, "what were the stakes of your wager?"

Artemis looked panicked.

"A kiss, Your Royal Highness," Orion lied, not taking his eyes from her. "We wagered a kiss."

The prince laughed. "Well then, Miss Rose, I think it is high time you paid your debt."

The crowd took up the call: "Yes, yes!" "Do collect, Lindenshire!" "Better hurry, Miss Rose, before the debt earns interest!"

Orion held Artemis's gaze for a moment before she gave an almost imperceptible nod and he bent his head to kiss her. His finger brushed her shoulders. She closed her eyes. Their lips met, pressed, and parted. Quick and emotionless. She bowed her head once more. The music resumed, and the people swarmed onto the dance floor

It was all over.

Couples twirled about them, smiling and talking.

Artemis was silent. And Orion felt dead inside.

"I will do as you have asked," she said quietly. "I will depart tomorrow. I"—she looked down at her hands— "I think I will go to Truro."

"So far away."

"Yes. I think it is best." She hesitated. "Don't you?"

He didn't answer her. Instead, he pulled her into his arms and swept her into the ring of waltzing couples. "One more dance," he said. "A dance between friends."

"Yes," she said with a tremulous smile. "We are still that."

"We always have been."

"And we always will be."

He held her close and whirled her round and round, clinging to the moment with a desperation he did not understand. Wasn't this what he wanted? She was wrong for him, wasn't she?

She was.

And yet, he wasn't happy. The last time he had been truly happy was when they were together as children, when he didn't have any interest in analyzing their relationship. He just knew he loved her and that he loved being with her. The years without her had been empty, and he didn't want to lose her a second time.

And then it hit him: he would rather lose the *ton's* regard than lose Artemis. She was all wrong for the part of him that chose not to wear his spectacles. She was all wrong for the dashing man who didn't know a beetle from an arachnid. But she wasn't wrong for the real Orion. That Orion didn't give a fig if people thought him odd. And that Orion would not let her go.

He pulled her to a halt. As couples danced around

them, throwing them curious stares, her eyes searched his. He caressed the side of her face and smiled wistfully. "Since you left, Gypsy . . . all those years . . . I searched for someone to accept me."

Her eyes flicked around them. "*They* accept you."

"No." He shook his head. "They accept the person I pretend to be." He put his other hand to her face and framed it. "I no longer care what they think."

"Oh, Orion," she murmured.

"You are perceptive, compassionate, empathetic, and clever. I do not want to lose you. I *will not* lose you."

She closed her eyes and, tipping her head, nuzzled his palm. Her dark, glossy hair felt like satin against his fingers. He rubbed his thumb against the back of her ear.

They were being openly stared at now, and Orion did not care. "You asked me once what it mattered if you had a place to live and a full belly if you did not have love."

"And?" she whispered.

"And I did not understand. But I do now. What does it matter if I have society's regard, if I do not have love?"

And then, there in the middle of the floor, Orion pulled his spectacles from his pocket and put them on.

"What are you doing?" she said in wonderment.

He smiled down at her and tucked an errant strand of her lovely hair behind one ear. "I wanted to see your face clearly when I asked you to marry me."

"What?"

He knelt at her feet and took her hand. Around them, the waltz came to a stop as the dancers stilled, round-eyed.

"Will you, my beloved friend, do me the honor of marrying me—the real me?" He held his breath. After the stupid way he had been acting the past three days— no! the past three months—he wouldn't blame her if she refused him. He searched her eyes, hoping.

And then, as the seconds stretched into centuries,

he did something illogical. Irrational. Irresistible. And, somehow, the thing that felt right.

Raising his hand and holding it close over his heart, the ultralogical Orion Chase crossed his fingers.

Her blue eyes followed the movement and widened, and her sudden smile branded its beauty and joy onto his soul. "Of course I will marry you, you goose."

Orion's heart soared, and he kissed her soundly. Around them, the room swelled with the startled reaction of the crowd. He took his time breaking the kiss. "Come," he said finally, leading her to the edge of the room. The crowd hastily parted to let them pass. He made directly for the Archbishop of Canterbury and bowed. "Would you grant me a special license, Your Grace?"

"After that kiss, how could I refuse, my son?" the white-haired man asked with a warmth that belied his stern expression. "Consider it granted, Lindenshire." He smiled. "You may marry whenever and wherever you wish."

The crowd applauded, and the prince laughed.

Orion turned to Artemis. "I do not believe in long engagements."

"Neither do I. When do you wish to wed?" she asked.

"Tonight. Right here in this ballroom. Right now," he answered her with a grin. "Can you think of a more logical time?"

# EPILOGUE

"Are you certain you do not mind about the north parlor?" Orion asked his bride.

"Not at all."

"But my equipment . . . you know it is visible through the windows?"

She laughed. "Orion, my love, stop fretting."

"I do not care who sees my laboratory, but I thought you might. I want everything to be perfect for you."

"Everything *is* perfect, Orion. We are wed, you are back to being you, I study the signs, and you study your bugs."

"When we are not studying each other, that is," Orion said, kissing her hand.

She laughed. "Ah, Orion . . . can you believe it? We are in love! Everything is perfect. All is as it should be—including your new laboratory. So stop worrying and enjoy the ball."

It was January the eighth, two days after Epiphany, and Orion and Artemis were attending their second ball as a married couple: Ophelia Robertson's, of course. Artemis looked radiant, and he wasn't sure which was pinker—her becomingly flushed cheeks or her vibrant pink gown.

Orion smiled and gave a shrug. "The north parlor has the best light in the house, and you need light for your embroidery."

"And you need light for your bugs. That is more important. The most logical thing to do is to leave your laboratory right where it is."

Orion smiled and, pulling her to him, gave her a long, heated kiss right there in the ballroom. Such displays of passion were not the fashionable thing to do, but he had found he did not give a damn. Loving Artemis was what he wanted to do, what made him happy to do. And, judging by the answering warmth and the smile in her eyes, it was the thing that made *her* happy, too, which was good enough for Orion.

"I will reserve a corner of my laboratory for your embroidery hoop and chiffonier," he said, "the one near the fire."

"You will not find my presence distracting?" she asked, turning her wedding rings round and round on her finger. Orion had replaced the original yellow gold ring with the white, but she insisted on wearing them both.

"Yes, I will no doubt be frightfully distracted," Orion said and gave her another passionate kiss.

True Sinclair approached. "Careful, Lindenshire, or everyone will begin to think your friendship with me has tainted your character."

Mrs. Robertson had invited her son and his wife to the ball, of course. Since he'd dropped his tonnish façade and gotten to know Truesdale Sinclair, Orion had found True to be an intelligent man of good character in spite of his rakish reputation. He was a worthy match for Marianna—and now a trusted friend of Orion's.

The Sinclairs—along with the Robertsons and Lord and Lady Blackshire—seemed more like family now than friends. They had all been spending a enormous amount of time together.

"Marianna is in the ladies' retiring room and needs some assistance with her gown," True told Artemis. "A little loosening of the stays, I think. Our child is asserting his presence rather early."

"Children." Artemis corrected True with a smile and quit the room.

"Did she say 'children'?" True asked, his expression incredulous.

"She did," Orion said, "but I would not place too much importance on her predictions. She has been wrong before, after all," he said, referring to her failure at their betrothal wager.

"Yes, well . . . Marianna certainly believes. I suppose influence has flowed in both directions."

"In *all* directions, more like," Orion said, nodding toward the end of the room, where Mrs. Robertson and her husband John presided over the ball from upon a dais—though they were paying less attention to the ball then they were to spoiling Anna dreadfully. But it was not those upon the dais his gaze rested upon, but those in the alcove just behind the dais. There his mother stood, talking quietly with her butler.

True nodded. "Think your mother is following in Ophelia Robertson's footsteps?" John Robertson had been a family servant for thirty years before he and Mrs. Robertson had run away to Gretna Green together.

Orion shook his head thoughtfully, "Perhaps . . . though I admit my mother was already rather free-thinking even before she and Ophelia became friends."

"Do you object to the match?" True asked.

"Peabody is a good man," Orion said. "I only hope they do not elope, as Ophelia and John did. The ladies would enjoy planning a spring wedding."

True laughed. "You have a gift for understatement. We would probably see precious little of our wives, your mama, or mine for weeks on end."

"Marianna and Artemis need little provocation to spend time together," Orion agreed.

The two young women had curled up for a long, comfortable coze in a parlor off the ballroom in Ophelia and John's grand house on Grosvenor Square, mostly ignoring the ball that was going on around them. The two of them were very alike in many ways, and they'd become bosom friends within an ace of their first meeting. It was destiny, they declared—a claim proved, they said, by the admittedly startling discovery the two of them had made concerning the stockings flung from the passing coach. They'd been discarded by none other than Marianna Sinclair herself. The outrageous stockings that played a part in bringing Orion and Artemis together had played a part in bringing True and Marianna together, too.

Artemis was insufferably pleased about it, for she felt it gave her assertion that the stockings' appearance at her feet had been a sign.

Of course, Orion knew it was just a very amazing coincidence. He still didn't believe in all of that Gypsy rubbish.

Hell and blast, if she were right and Marianna Sinclair did carry twins, he'd never hear the end of it.

The rest of the evening passed in a happy blur of dancing and laughter. Artemis passed some of the time reading palms and making predictions, but Orion only smiled indulgently. No, he still didn't believe in signs or palm lines, or other such superstitious rot—but he did believe in the magical power of love to overcome a couple's incompatibility.

"I love to dance with you," he told her as they waltzed. "I have never been happier than I am now."

Artemis looked into Orion's eyes—through the glass

of his spectacles—and knew what he said was true. She loved Orion with all her heart. She always had, and now he loved her, too. "Destiny is not as bad as it sounded, is it, my love?"

The sly jab earned her a shake of his head and a sidelong smile.

At last, the Sir Roger de Coverley was called, supper was taken, and at the end of the meal, Mrs. Robertson stood up with a flourish and a wave of her hand. "I know Prinny spoiled the announcement," she said, "but a wager is a wager, and a promise is a promise. I promised to give Lord and Lady Lindenshire this ball, and I have—though I did not think it would come after their wedding!"

Scattered applause and congratulations forced a pause.

"And now," Ophelia announced, "it is time to open the envelopes and find out just how far off Lady Lindenshire's guess was."

Artemis smiled as Orion toasted her good nature. "She really has been a good sport about her loss," he said, smiling.

"As everyone knows," Ophelia continued, "the number of couples betrothed was seventeen. Lindenshire," she said, slitting one envelope and reading the enclosed card, "guessed sixteen, while his bride"—she pulled forth the other envelope and wrinkled her brow—"guessed *seventeen!*" She turned the card over for everyone to see. "Seventeen!"

Beside her, Orion looked stunned. "You won?"

At one end of the table, Ophelia cackled and rose. "Supper is over. Games and punch in the parlor, for anyone who will stay."

A few of the guests departed for home, but the company was merry, and many were unwilling to leave, even at that late hour. They crowded the parlor playing conundrums, my lady's slipper, and pantomimes and taking turns playing the pianoforte and singing. To

Artemis's delight, Orion consented to play the harp if she would sing along, which she did, joyfully.

Finally, just as the rosy fingers of the sun had begun to illumine the edge of the blue bowl of the sky, Orion took her hand and tugged her onto the privacy of the terrace. It had rained, and the air was crisp and sweet-smelling with the perfume of dawn.

"Why?" he asked.

"Hmm?" she said with a deliberately mischievous grin.

"You know very well what I am asking," he said. "Why did you deliberately let me—and everyone else—believe I had won the wager?"

Artemis gave him a gentle smile. "To wed was our destiny, but you had to see that for yourself, or you would not have been happy."

"Destiny!" Orion scoffed lovingly. "Superstitious rubbish. It was love that brought us together," he said. "Love, pure and simple—which ought to bring you some consolation," he said with a chuckle, "since I, Lord Logic, will own that love is not logical in the least."

She laughed and, taking his strong hand in hers, kissed his long, sensitive fingers and then looked up at him.

"Your eyes are full of mischief," he said, plucking a fragrant pink rose from an arrangement and tucking it behind her ear. "What devilry is in your head?"

"I have been waiting for the right time." She raised her delicate, lace-edged pink sleeve and pulled from it the faded, water-stained wish envelope. Without a word, she offered it to him.

Slowly, carefully, he opened it and pulled out the card inside. There, scrawled in a childish hand, were the words she had written so long ago:

*I wish that Orion Chase will fall in love with me and that we shall be wed.*

"You are not going to let me forget this, are you?" he asked.

"Never in a thousand years," she answered happily. "Never in a thousand years."

## About the Author

Melynda Beth Skinner was born in 1963 in Florida, where she still lives with her husband of twelve years and their charming hellions, two logical little girls who wouldn't dream of crossing their fingers. She enjoys hearing from readers.

Visit her online at www.melyndbethskinner.com, where you can send her an e-mail or chat with her online. Or you can write to her at 7259 Aloma Avenue, Suite 2, Box 31, Winter Park, FL 32792.

Please enclose a SASE if you wish a reply.

If you liked this story, you may also enjoy the author's first and second novels. *The Blue Devil* and *Miss Grantham's One True Sin* are connected to *Lord Logic and the Wedding Wish* in some surprising ways— including appearances by the outrageous and clever Ophelia Robertson.

Next in this connected series will be *The Blackguard's Bride,* which features George DeMoray—the villain from this novel you're holding!—as hero.